CAZ REDPATH

Read My Rights

Editing by Hannah G. Scheffer-Wentz, English Proper Editing Services

First edition

This book was professionally typeset on Reedsy.
Find out more at reedsy.com

To all those hiding their pain in the dark. I see you, I hope this story brings you comfort.

You deserve to live happily ever after too.

"We all have a voice. Some a whisper, some a roar.

If you can roar, roar for others.

If you can only whisper, keep trying. Every roar started small."

-M.L. SHANAHAN

Contents

Content Warnings

Read My Rights contains references to the following topics:

- Grief and Loss
- Domestic Violence
- Anxiety
- Murder

One

Elijah

15 Years Earlier

I had always been a light sleeper.

According to Ma, it drove her up the wall when I was little as I was constantly waking up in the night. Tonight was no exception as the sound of footsteps had my eyes open of their own accord. I laid there and listened for a moment, feeling slightly anxious at the sound. I'd come to know the sounds of my family members' footsteps and these sounded different. I sat up slowly, but I couldn't seem to get myself out of bed. I was frozen. *Was there someone else in my house?* I tried to get myself to get up, but I couldn't. My heart was pounding and I was scared. Logically, I knew I needed to get up and investigate the source of the noise to make sure it wasn't just me over-reacting. I sat quietly listening and heard the footsteps retreating back down the stairs. They definitely

1

were not ones I recognised.

I stood up and my hand hovered over my door knob, but I couldn't bring myself to turn it. I don't know how long I stood there before I heard my parents' door open. The sound of my father's footsteps was now following the original set down the stairs. A large crash prompted me to grab the door and yank it open. I ran down the stairs, closely followed by my mother.

In the front room my father had his hands in the air. His eyes widened with panic as I came into view. My eyes were then drawn to a man in a balaclava in front of him, holding a gun up.

"Look, there is some cash in my office. If I give it to you, will you go?" Despite the predicament he was in, my dad's voice was calm and collected. He was a criminal defence lawyer, so he was used to remaining calm, but still his ability to remain so calm in a high-pressured situation amazed me.

"The boy can get it, you stay there." My dad looked over to me and then my mother who was hovering on the stairs.

"Go get it, Eli." I didn't need to be told twice. I turned and ran into my father's office around the corner. I knew he kept the cash in his bottom drawer, so I quickly pulled it out before returning. I paused then when I got back into the room, unsure of whether to approach the armed intruder or not.

"Bring it." The man's voice was harsh, but I could still sense some panic in it; like he was just as unsure about what he was doing as the rest of us.

"Let me hand it to you," my father interjected.

"No, he brings it."

At those words I cautiously moved forward, holding the money out as far as I could. He snatched it off me with one hand whilst keeping the gun pointed at my father. I felt my whole body shaking. He raised his hand, smacking me across the face and knocking me to the floor.

"How dare you!" My father's voice boomed behind me as I heard him get closer. A split second later, the sound of a gunshot filled the room alongside my mother's screams. I heard the thud as my father fell backwards onto the ground. "James!" my mother screamed as she made her way over to him.

I looked up, my eyes staring at the intruder who looked terrified at his own actions. He was staring down at his gun like he wasn't the one who just set it off. As his eyes met mine, he turned and darted out the front door. I found my way to my feet, crashing through the door behind him.

"Elijah!" my mother screamed after me. "Elijah, stop!" Her desperate cries fell on deaf ears. I had no intention of stopping as I chased the man down the street. He could have turned and shot me at any moment, but he didn't. He carried on running, tipping any object standing in the street to slow me down. My heart was racing as we continued down the street. I felt like I was getting closer to him, almost to a point where I could reach out and grab the back of his shirt. I suddenly felt my foot get caught in a gap in the sidewalk, throwing me forward face-down with a crash. By the time I gathered myself back up again, the man was no longer in sight. I raced round the corner, but he wasn't there, either. *I'd lost him.* I stood for a few moments, hoping he would appear again, but it was no good. He was long gone. I turned and raced back to my house to find multiple emergency vehicles littered outside. I pushed past one of the officers outside and back into my house where I saw my father still on the ground, surrounded by his own blood. I could hear the sound of his voice weakly speaking to my mother as the paramedics pulled out equipment from their bag. I moved closer and crouched by his side, taking his hand in mine.

"You're not allowed to leave me. You know that don't you?" my mother said between sobs. "You promised me we'd spend our retirement driving the RV round the country." I felt tears fall from my own eyes as I squeezed his hand tight, but he was giving nothing back. It was obvious his strength was fading. I watched as the paramedics started to inspect the wound, knowing soon I'd be pushed out of the way so they could move him.

"Do you remember what I told you when we got married?" His voice was weak and his words came out slowly. "I told you I hoped I went before you," he coughed, interrupting his sentence, "because I couldn't live a day without you, Lucy." My mother's sobs increased in volume.

"Not yet, please." I was suddenly aware of a police officer ushering my siblings back up the stairs, both looking frightened as they watched. My father didn't reply to my mother, but she continued to plead with him. I watched as his eyes closed and his breathing started to slow. The paramedics were pushing past us to get to him. There were lots of words spoken, but I wasn't taking any of them in. All I could do was watch as they started chest compressions. Frantic voices rang as I felt arms wrap around my waist, pulling me further out of the way. I turned to see my father's friend, Officer Daines, behind me.

"We need to get you out of the way, buddy, so they can help your dad, okay?" His voice was shaky as he continued to hold onto me. The next moments were a blur until I heard one of the paramedics say, "We are going to have to call it." The other stopped the compressions and my mother screamed.

"No!" I shouted, fighting to escape Daines' grip. But he held on tighter, wrestling me to the ground. "No, please! Don't stop!" I cried out.

But it was hopeless.

My father was dead and I did nothing to stop it.

This was all my fault.

Two

Elijah

Present Day

The faster my feet moved the more distance I was able to put between myself and the thoughts in my head. My body called out for me to slow down but I couldn't allow it to. I couldn't allow the thoughts to consume me. Not now.

It was still early and I forced myself to focus on the sunrise as I continued to place one foot in front of the other. Eventually I allowed myself to give in to a slower pace as the trail started to become uphill. I ran these routes almost every day, but I couldn't shake the feeling that I needed to start making it harder.

If it became too easy I would get complacent. Complacency was a one-way ticket to failure, which was not an option for me. I couldn't allow weakness to consume me.

I *wouldn't* allow it.

A piercing scream broke my trance. I couldn't make out the words, but the fear in the scream sent shivers down my spine. *Where was it coming from?*

I spun myself round, looking for the source of the scream. I couldn't see anyone, but I could still hear it. It sounded like it was coming from my left so I turned off the path and ran towards the noise. Fear threatened to overwhelm me but I pushed it down, quickening my pace towards the source of the scream.

It was getting louder; I had to be getting closer.

I ran as fast as I physically could towards it. I needed to get there. I needed to help her. I cursed myself for not bringing my gun out with me on runs.

As the scream threatened to deafen me, I stopped briefly to look around. I still couldn't place it. "Where are you?" I shouted out, but there was no reply.

All of a sudden, the screaming stopped and a silence scarier than the scream filled the air. It was so quiet I could hear my own heart beating violently against my chest.

"I'm here, tell me where you are. I can help!" I yelled out again. No response.

"Elijah?" A questioning voice called from behind.

I turned quickly to see Jake, our neighbour making his way over to me. "Are you okay? I heard you shouting." He raised a concerned brow at me as he stopped. I took a second to catch my breath before responding.

"I heard someone screaming, I'm trying to find out where they are." My head was still searching around. It was quiet now, but I listened for any sound of movement. Anything that would give me an indication as to where she was.

"Really? I didn't hear anything; I just ran down the trail alongside here," he said, pointing. "The only noise I've heard was you."

I allowed my eyes to stop searching and meet his. His words felt heavy as I digested them. Those screams were so loud, he was running right where they were coming from. How did he not hear them?

The truth dawned on me then. *The screams were not real.*

I had allowed it to take control. Again. My mind was playing tricks on me. *Again.*

The screams were nothing but an old memory.

"I must have been hearing things, I didn't get much sleep last night," I joked, trying to play off my embarrassment. I knew better than to let myself fall into this trap. I needed to pull myself together. "Sorry for interrupting your run."

"Don't worry, the wind can play tricks up here." A kind smile formed on Jake's lips.

If he thought I was crazy, he wasn't showing it on his face. "Are you heading this way? Want to finish up together?"

Truthfully, I couldn't face any more conversation after that, so I lied. "Actually, I'm going to head down there, but I'm sure I'll see you later." He gave me a quick nod before heading off on his own run again.

My lie had just extended my morning run by a couple more miles. I would be paying for that later.

When I eventually returned home, I wasted no time in getting in the shower post run. I slowly turned the temperature hotter and hotter until it was scalding my skin. It was a bad habit of mine, but I wanted the shower to burn. I wanted that reminder that I was still here, that I could still feel something.

If it were up to me I would have stayed there for hours, but after getting side tracked on my run I didn't have as much time as usual before work. I put on my uniform and headed out the door. I wasn't in the mood to make myself anything, so another café breakfast it was. It looked like my brother hadn't bothered to make himself anything on the way out, either. It felt like he was up and out earlier each day at the moment. I pulled out my phone and shot him a text.

E: Dinner at Blake's later?

I felt protective over both my siblings being the oldest, like I had a responsibility to keep an eye on them and make sure they were taking care of themselves. My brother was putting his all into his business and I was proud of him, but I couldn't help but worry about him. He was going to burn himself out soon if he didn't take a minute to slow down. If nothing else, I could make sure he got one decent meal in him today.

The coffee shop I frequented was called Caffeine Central, a fitting name since caffeine seemed to be the centre of the universe for a lot of the patrons.

It was located directly opposite the police station where I worked and was extremely popular amongst the officers. Honestly, it was really the only reason I ate properly most days.

"Coffee with the breakfast special?" Jane asked almost as soon as I walked through the door. She was the owner and always talked about slowing down. But every time I saw her, she seemed to be working harder and faster.

"You know me well. Thank you, J." I probably should be embarrassed to be known that well, but it was comforting. Jane was one of those people who not only asked how you were, but she was genuinely interested in the answer. She was also one of the only people I could stand small talk with. "You have any luck with your vacancy?" I asked. She shook her head.

"No, but I could do with filling the position soon. I know I have Maggie, and she's great, but I'm hoping one of these days I can work a few less hours myself. I shouldn't complain; you officers are always keeping me busy. I appreciate that, I'm just not getting any younger," she laughed, busying herself with the coffee machine.

"Who would have thought opening a coffee shop opposite a police station would be a hit?" I teased. "I'll keep an ear to the ground. If I hear anyone looking, I'll send them your way."

"Thank you." She smiled softly. "You've always been one of my favourites Officer Weatherston." She winked at me as she handed me my coffee and breakfast sandwich. "I'm sure the perfect person will waltz into town and land in my lap soon enough."

I nodded to her and made my way over to one of the tables near the back of the café.

It was early, but it wouldn't be long until this place was swarmed with locals.

I still had some time before my shift started. As much as I regretted leaving the blistering shower as quickly as I did, it was nice to have a moment of peace now. I sat down and placed my bits on the table. I couldn't help but watch the front of the station out the window. People watching was almost second nature to me now. I was always wondering what people were doing and where they were going. I couldn't help sometimes wondering if they were up to anything bad.

Was that man walking fast because he was late or was he

running away from something he'd done? I was consumed by my obsession with social observation.

I guess in a way it was my job to look for malicious intentions and uphold the law, but there was an intensity in the way I watched the world. I felt like I couldn't ever switch off, not for a single moment. What if I wasn't paying attention and someone got hurt? If I wasn't watching, then who was? I needed to keep my wits about me. It wasn't a want—it was a necessity.

I felt the world on my shoulders.

If I made one wrong move, then the whole thing would fall apart. I couldn't help but catastrophize.

My chest tightened with each movement outside as a sense of guilt washed over me. Guilt that I wasn't out there stopping these bad things from happening.

A buzz from my phone distracted me briefly from the nerves bubbling away in my stomach. Or it may have been hunger as I had yet to touch my sandwich.

L: *Only if you're paying*

Asshole.

My brother's business was successful enough that he could definitely afford his own dinner, but as my younger brother he had this need to irritate me as much as possible. He would likely spend the entire dinner ripping me a new one about something or other before chucking me the check at the end. I sighed and sent him a thumbs up emoji in return. I couldn't complain too much—it was my idea. It was the only way to make sure he finished at a decent time today. He'd work late into the night if I let him. Being a workaholic seemed to run in the family.

Putting my phone back in my pocket, I tucked into my sandwich, taking my attention away from the window. I would spend all shift watching people I could take a minute away from it—at least that's what I told myself. As soon as I finished, I turned my attention to my coffee. I wasn't *completely* lying to Jake earlier when I said I hadn't slept very well last night. I never slept well; I could never shut my brain long enough to allow for much sleep.

The café door opened with a clang as Officers Lawrence and Taylor entered. Their laughter filled the previously peaceful and quiet café. They had this obnoxious aura around them as they approached Jane. *That's my cue to leave.* I quickly finished the dregs of my coffee.

"Elijah!"

The booming voice of Daniel Taylor pierced through my peace.

"You got time for another coffee?" His eyes darted between myself and Jane. I did indeed have time for another coffee; however, I'd rather stick pins in my eyes then spend a minute longer than I needed to in their company.

"Sorry, in a rush. Another time, maybe." I didn't leave them enough time to respond as I made my way out the door. I crossed the street to the station.

I guess I will be clocking in a little early today.

Three

Charlotte

After loading the last of the bags into the trunk, I took a moment to watch the sunrise. There was something beautiful in watching the light begin to overwhelm the dark sky that had been there before. If you had told me a few hours ago that this night would end, I wouldn't have believed you. I felt like I had been trapped in the darkness, that I would never see the sun again.

Yet here it is, breaking through the night time into a new day. For the first time in a long time, a new day was a good thing. It meant I had a chance to make it better. This time there was a hope in that light and I was going to cling onto it for as long as it would allow. A sense of anxiety washed over me but I tried to push it down. I felt like I had spent so long scared, frightened of what he would do to me. I didn't know how to feel anything else.

He left an hour ago to head to some bar or other, giving me

a brief period to make a plan. I knew I didn't have long. He was probably watching me right now on the cameras. I had to hope he was too drunk to piece together anything. The last few weeks has his control tightening. The frequency in which he came home filled with rage was on the rise. Rage that he took out on me. I'm not going to wait around for him to start taking it out on our son. If we don't leave now, tomorrow could be too late. For both of us.

I took a deep breath in, keeping my eyes to the sky for one final moment before stepping into the car. I pulled out the paper with the hotel address written on it and placed it into my navigation. It would be a few hours of driving before we got there, but it'd be worth it.

"Ready to go on our adventure?" I asked, turning to Theo in the backseat. He gave me a slightly lopsided thumbs up as his eyes were still half closed. I watched as he nestled his head into the side of his car seat before I turned the car on and pulled away.

I can do this. We can do this. Everything will be okay. It has to be.

A couple of hours later I was still repeating those words in my head over and over. We'd stopped for breakfast and got back on the highway not too far from our destination. The darkness was completely gone now and the sun shone bright in the sky. Summer was well underway.

Theo briefly woke up at the promise of food, but had drifted off again almost as soon as we had gotten back in the car. Neither of us exactly got any sleep last night, so I didn't blame him. Truthfully, I was enjoying the quiet. I was running purely on caffeine, fear, and desperation to get to the hotel to rest. To keep me and my son safe. I was looking forward to a peaceful day before the hard work started tomorrow. Trying not to think about my ever growing to do list, I turned up the volume on my car speakers.

The harmonic tones of Billy Joel's *Piano Man* filled the space in the car.

This was one of my favourite CDs to play and truthfully, it was the third time I had gone through it on this drive alone.

Almost involuntarily, I took a deep breath.

My body desperately tried to inhale the peace of the moment, as if somehow it would help calm my brain down. As a way of blocking my mind out, I allowed myself to get too lost in the song.

I hummed along to the music, careful not to be too loud and wake Theo. It was my grandpa who first introduced me to Billy Joel. *Just The Way You Are* had been a firm favourite of my grandparents. I was suddenly transported into the memory of dancing around the living room with him.

When I was little there was always music at their house. It was always so loud and vibrant, just like the people that lived there. It was something I carried into my adulthood; I couldn't stand the quiet. When things were too quiet it made my mind wander. Or it meant danger was around the corner.

Everything would be okay as long as there was music playing.

My grandpa was someone who on the outside looked stern and serious, but on the inside he was a kind man. He dedicated his life to his family and their happiness.

He always did whatever he could to put a smile on my face and he was good at it. I loved going to their house. Truthfully, it felt more like home to me than my parents' house ever did.

His prized possession was his piano. Watching his fingers

move along the keys was like magic to me. It was effortless and beautiful. I found myself mesmerised watching him as a little girl. His music was like a river flowing elegantly. He rarely used sheet music; he had been playing so long his fingers just knew what to do.

As a child I was in awe of him. Nobody could come close to him. He was my hero.

I was only about eleven when my grandma died, it happened suddenly. One day she was here and the next we had gotten a call to say she passed away in her sleep. There had been no warnings, no long-drawn-out illness; she was just gone. We went to visit my grandpa that day and it was the first time I'd walked into that house and it was silent. There was no Billy Joel playing, he wasn't at his piano, and he didn't try to make me laugh once.

In the years between grandma's death and his own, music never played in that house again. I never so much as saw him sit at that piano. He had tried to teach me when I was younger, so when we visited I tried to play. Granted, I was terrible, but I thought it might just convince him to play something better. He never so much as even looked my way.

When I was fourteen, I got angry at him. His silence felt like a personal attack on me. Where had the man gone that once stopped at nothing to make those around him happy? Who was this fragile shell of a man that we were left with? It wasn't fair. I needed him and he wasn't there anymore. It felt like he may as well have been dead, too.

He only met my anger with silence. Silence that matched that of the unrecognisable atmosphere in the once lively house. He offered no explanation. He simply looked right through me. I stopped visiting of my own accord then, only going

16

when I was forced to by my parents. My parents both worked away so often that previously my grandparents had looked after me, but I was old enough now I didn't need a babysitter. I opted to stay at home rather than sit in that miserable silence.

He died just over two years later. I'd only seen him a couple of times since my outburst and he'd appeared frailer each time. I was still angry at him even then for shutting me out, but it didn't stop my heart from breaking when I was told he passed. The anger and grief sat side by side in my heart, constantly shifting me between tears and resentment.

We cleared out his house a couple of weeks later. I found a box of old sheet music and insisted my mum let me have it. I couldn't play, but it was important to me to keep it. I didn't win the argument about keeping the piano. It shattered me when I watched it be carried away by strangers. That was his piano—no one else deserved to let their fingers touch those keys.

Among his things we found a letter addressed to me, well, with his nickname for me. *Little Charlie* was written on the front of it. Nobody else called me Charlie but him. My parents used my full name, Charlotte, and a few friends called me Lottie. Truthfully, I loved his nickname. It was our thing and always made me feel special.

I still had the letter now; it sat in an envelope in my handbag on the passenger seat. I read it over and over again when I first got it before putting it away in a box. I couldn't bring myself to throw it away. I knew one day I would need it again.

Last night was that night. I read it for the first time in years because I needed his advice. I knew everything I needed to know was in his words.

*** *

To My Little Charlie,

If you are reading this then I am no longer here.

I have been getting sicker over the past year and I didn't want to go without writing to you. Please don't blame your mother, I insisted she keep my illness a secret. I know that our relationship has faced hardship and it is because of me. You are in high school now with new friends and hobbies. I did not want you to waste your precious time on a sick, sad, old man. I want nothing more than for you to live life to the fullest.

I haven't been who you needed me to be for the past couple of years and I'm sorry. I don't blame you for one moment for stopping to visit me. If you still were, I'd be telling you to stop myself. My grief and misery are painted all over the walls here. I can feel it seeping out constantly. I wouldn't want it to consume you as it has me.

Please don't feel sad for me that I am gone, I do not want your pity or your guilt. Truthfully, I am happy to be dying, for in death I get to be with your grandma again. There is not a moment that goes by that my body doesn't ache to be near her. The world hasn't felt right since she left me.

I don't think I ever told you the story of how we met and I wanted to make sure you knew. It's important to me that you understand all of it.

I learned to play piano when I was a boy; my mother insisted. She had always played and wanted at least one of her children to carry it on. I hated it. I wanted to play sports and that was all I cared about. I gave it up as soon as I could.

Your grandma, my Lily, lived in one of the houses across the street. I had observed her from a distance but I was too scared to ask her out. Eventually, I plucked up the courage to speak to her and that weekend we made plans to attend a local place that did live music on Saturdays. I was a bag of nerves for the whole rest of the week.

From the beginning I could tell she was enamoured with the music. She watched them while I watched her. There was pure joy in her face, there wasn't a single hint of sadness in her smile. It was in that moment I realised I wanted to be the reason she smiled like that; I would do whatever it took to make her happy.

We had a great evening; I asked her questions about all the music she enjoyed and walked her home on my arm. The next day I went to the music shop and bought sheet music to all her favourite artists. I still had my old piano.

My mother was under the impression I still played and insisted I took it with me when I moved out. I didn't have the heart to tell her I didn't play anymore and it was just collecting dust in the living room.

I spent weeks learning all these songs. I was rusty, but it quickly felt like no time had passed. In the meantime, we had a few more dates and I was falling hard for her. The harder I fell the more I played. Eventually we attended the same live music night we went to on our first date. Except this time, there was an additional act. She was so confused when I got up and started walking towards the stage. I played a handful of her favourite songs. I had purposely practised them so much that I hardly needed to look at the keys. I wanted to look at her when I played, I wanted to see her smile. The smile that I was putting there. I asked her to marry me that night and made a promise to myself that I would spend my life making her smile.

She's gone. I will never be able to make her smile ever again. I didn't play because I loved playing, I played because I loved her. Why would I play now if she isn't here to smile?

I wanted you to know this story for two reasons.

Firstly, to understand why I have been quiet since she left. Why the piano keys have remained untouched and will remain untouched by my hands. The next time I will play is when I am reunited with her. I will play to make her smile once more.

The second reason is I want you to promise me something, Charlie. You are special and I do not want you to settle for any less than you deserve.

Someday someone will love you like I loved Lily; they will do anything to make you happy. You will mean the absolute world to them and they will live for your smile. They will fight for your smile.

One day, one of you will die and it will be earth shattering, but it will be okay. It will be okay because you loved them and they loved you. You lived every day together feeling loved and seen. How lucky you will be to have been loved and to be able to love. It will be okay because you made the most of every moment together.

Promise me you won't settle for anything less. Life is too short to not be loved in the way you deserve.

I'm so proud of you, Charlie,

Grandpa x

* * *

When I was little, I told my grandma I wanted to grow up and marry a man just like grandpa. The truth is, I don't know if that will ever happen. I've never met a man like him. I've never known how it feels to be loved like that.

Instead, I felt like I had betrayed this promise–I had done the exact opposite. I had been so desperate to be loved, I had found myself with someone who showed how he felt about me through fear and control. Wasting precious years cowering in a corner because I had nowhere to go. I know if my grandpa was here, he would never have let this happen.

Theo and I would be safe with him. There was nobody in our corner now and it was up to me to be brave and take care of us both.

I broke off from the memory with fresh tears rolling down my cheeks. I quickly wiped them as I hit my turn signal to pull off the highway. I glanced in the mirror and watched the highway get smaller and smaller.

The road got quieter and quieter.

Silence.

It wouldn't be long until we got there now.

Four

Elijah

I go through the motions, completing the pre-shift checks on my patrol car. I've crossed the t's and dotted the i's hundreds of times. My car has never failed to be exactly as it needed to be. However, I'm not naïve. I know it only takes one mistake, one careless day for something to go seriously wrong. In a job like mine, that mistake can be the difference between life or death. My life or someone else's.

So, I check my list and I check it again. When I first started in the force, I used to check it three times, but I've convinced myself now that two is sufficient. There is such a thing as overkill, I discovered. I ignored the anxious feeling creeping up my neck as I put the clipboard down and climbed into the car. Usually, I go out on patrol with Officer Daines, but he's away visiting family. I refuse to go out with anyone else. It was an argument I happily had with my superiors and they eventually relented. I didn't shy away from confrontation.

Officer Jack Daines understands my ways and the importance of being thorough in how we go about our work. He's worked on the force a long time and was good friends with my father. Since that night that changed my life, we became closer. I've always felt safe in his presence and I hoped he felt the same in mine. It was important to have someone you trusted by your side.

The same can't be said for others in my department. Officers Lawrence and Taylor were two examples of officers who believed they were above it all. They allowed their egos to fuel their reactions. The people of Rosehaven deserved better than that.

The name *rose* to me should be a reminder of the beauty of the town and all that it represented. It was a small town, but the people took care of it. They were the ones who made it beautiful. A *haven* was supposed to be a safe place, a place of refuge. For the most part, the people were safe here. Crime rates weren't what they were in the cities, that was for sure.

However, I don't remember the last time I felt truly safe here and the beauty of this town faded fifteen years ago. It was a constant reminder of all of the mistakes I had ever made. I had debated moving several times, but I could never bring myself to take that step. This was my home. Even if it didn't feel like it anymore.

I became a police officer to feel like I had some control. I want to make the town safe, to keep the people safe. My family still lived here, too. I would protect them and this town until I couldn't do it anymore. I guess that's why I couldn't move–the people I loved the most were here and they needed me.

I wondered what it felt like to feel safe. I'd felt it once, hadn't I? My parents had always made me feel safe when I was small.

I feel like I walked through the first stages of my life with my eyes closed. But then one day they opened and I saw the world for what it truly was.

The darkness, the sadness, the evil all came right into view. I tried to close my eyes again, but they wouldn't. I was desperate to go back to the way it was. I wanted to feel safe again, but no matter how hard I tried to close my eyes, they would never stay shut. I couldn't block the memories out.

If I couldn't feel safe, then I would make sure everybody else did. That was my duty, that was why I was here. Maybe one day I would finally catch the feeling I'd been chasing.

I pulled the car out of the station and started making my way around the local streets. I didn't like sitting and waiting for a call. It wasn't that I went out of my way looking for trouble, I wasn't like that. I just felt better if I did a more active patrol, so that if and when a call came in, I was ready. A lot of the officers would park up somewhere and just wait all shift. That wasn't in my nature. I moved around for nearly an hour before I finally pulled in for a break.

We lived in a quiet town so there was really no major need to be as active as I was, but I couldn't help it. Sometimes I had to remind myself to take a step back and just breathe. I was getting better at it, or at least that's what I told myself. Every day I took another step forward, a step further away from the past and to hopefully a better future.

A call over the radio broke my thoughts–two teenagers had been caught stealing at the local grocery store. Likely they were kids from the next town over.

The small towns kids weren't stupid enough to steal from their own, mostly because everyone knew their name and faces so they'd never get away with it. Kids always went a town or two over to cause trouble.

"Officer Weatherston here, received and on route there now, over." I barely let them finish explaining the situation before I answered and drove around the corner. Luckily, I was only about two minutes away and the streets were quiet, so no reason for sirens.

I would be lying if I said I wasn't a bit disappointed to not get to use them; there was somewhat of an adrenaline rush when you had them on. Maybe I wasn't so different from the other officers driven by egos, after all.

As I got out of the car, I could see the two teenagers arguing with the shop assistant just inside the door. The assistant took up the threshold of the door, blocking their exit. Upon seeing me, the shop assistant turned and unlocked the door, opening it to let me in.

"Right, why don't you two—" The boys came barrelling past me, knocking me over and running down the high street. I cursed as I got up and started to run after them.

As I was closing the gap, one of them diverted off to the left. I had no choice but to pick one and go after them. I carried on straight, hoping I'd picked the slower of the two. I was just about to reach my hand out to grab the back of his shirt when I felt a shooting pain go through my leg as I fell to the ground.

"Fuck," was the only word I could muster as I grabbed my leg. Fucking cramp. I tried to get myself to my feet, but couldn't put weight properly on the leg and ended up back on the ground. By the time I was back standing, the boy was nowhere to be seen. I had lost him.

I had overdone it on my run and I had lost him. I hadn't worked hard enough. I wasn't good enough. I was letting everyone down. I'd made another mistake. I had taken my eye off the ball. I wasn't good enough. I was never going to be good enough.

The words swam round my head as I tried to shake them off.

"FUCK!" I shouted louder this time.

"For fuck's sake!" I yelled as I kicked a bin across the alley.

One kick wasn't enough to satisfy my rage. I kicked it again and again, trying to expel the anger out of my body. I kicked it until it was dented and the pain was back in my leg.

I took a breath and made my way back to the shop to take statements. I still had a job to do.

I drove around for a while after I finished taking statements. I was hoping to get lucky and come across the two boys. I knew it was stupid–there was no way they would hang around after that, but I couldn't stop myself. I couldn't let it go. The rage still consumed me.

Eventually, I made myself give up. I could no longer ignore the rumbling of my stomach that told me it was lunch time. I picked something up from the drive-thru before heading to the outskirts of town. If I stayed down town, I wouldn't be able to stop looking for them. I needed a break; I needed some quiet to calm down. My foul mood was infesting my space.

After pulling over on the side of the road, I pushed my head back and allowed my eyes to shut for a brief moment. Take deep breaths, that's what the website had said, hadn't it? I inhaled through my nose, only opening my eyes once I exhaled through my mouth. I did this a few more times hoping to feel a sense of calm, but it never came. I could still feel the anger running through me. I guess this bad mood was here to stay.

I ate my lunch in the quiet, I didn't like to have music playing in the car whilst I was working. I found it too distracting. Just as I was about to get out to stretch my legs, I heard a car coming from behind. I watched as it passed, noticing the broken tail light as they slowed for a hole in the road.

I don't know whether I was driven by my bad mood or my meticulous nature, but I put my car into drive and started heading towards them. As I got close, I flashed my siren briefly, letting them know I was pulling them over. They made no attempt to pull to the side.

"Pull over," I muttered under my breath as I flashed the siren once more, waiting for their response. Nothing. They still made no attempt to start slowing down or pull to the side.

I felt that adrenaline push through as I readied myself for a chase. I've signalled them twice and nothing.

I turned on my siren again, but this time I kept it on, moving my vehicle closer to theirs in an attempt to get them to pull over.

A few moments passed and still they still made no attempt to move off to the side.

"I'm not in the mood for this." I hit my fist on the wheel hard in frustration. Just as I was reaching for my radio to call for backup, they swung off to the side and parked.

I pulled in behind them and got out of the car, slamming my door behind me. I was fucking pissed.

Five

Charlotte

I switched the music over to the radio and turned the volume up as the latest pop hits played through. Theo was awake now and being entertained by his iPad, so I allowed the sound of music to fill the car. We weren't far out now, but I could feel my body crying out for some sleep or at least for me to lay down for a while. I needed the songs to keep me awake for just a little bit longer. I let myself feel every beat and vibration, willing myself to keep driving.

I heard Theo laugh as I sang louder, rolling the window down to let the breeze run through me. I felt happy. I couldn't help but grow a smile on my face.

I can do this. We can do this. We're safe.

Those words found their way back into my head, except this time, I really felt like that was the truth. Everything was going to get better from here on out.

I rolled my window back up but kept singing along as we

continued down the road. My eyes flicked up to the mirror and suddenly all I could see were flashing lights. As I turned down the music the sound of a siren filled my ears.

"Shit!" They were so close to me, how hadn't I seen it? I quickly swung off to the side, putting the car in park.

"Shit, shit, shit," I cursed, turning the engine off.

"Bad word!" Theo shouted from the backseat.

"Yes, thank you, Theo," my voice shook as I responded to him. How long had the police car been behind me? It can't have been that long, I would have seen. Why are they pulling me over, anyway? I was going the speed limit, wasn't I? I cursed myself for getting distracted by our music and singing.

A slam of the car door behind me broke me out of my thoughts. I quickly pulled the folder with my information out of the side door and rolled the window down in anticipation of their approach. My heart felt like it was going to beat right out of my chest as I fumbled with the buttons.

"Licence and registration." The tone of the officer's voice made me jump as he approached. His voice was gruff, and by the look on his face, you'd think I just punched his mother.

"Is there a problem, officer?" My voice trembles. I could feel my hands shaking as I held out my information. He snatched it with a low growl as he looked at my licence, his other hand gripping on tightly to my door.

"I've been trying to get you to pull over for half a mile. Are you blind or just stupid?" His voice was slightly lower now, but I could feel the anger in his tone.

He must have been exaggerating; there's no way he's been following me for that long. I'd pulled over as soon as I heard him. I don't even know why he pulled me over. I tried to study his face, but his hat covered most of it as he wrote down my details. I couldn't help but feel vulnerable. I had just left one angry man and seemed to immediately come face to face with another.

"I didn't see you, I pulled over as soon as I did." My instincts kicked in and I kept my tone soft in response in the hopes that it would calm him down. I know better than to match a hostile tone, I learned that the hard way.

My chest feel tight. I could feel the fear rising up inside of me. His head suddenly snapped away from his pad as his eyes met mine.

Even with his hard stare, there was a softness to his brown eyes. He was staring so intently I couldn't keep my gaze off of him. He ran a hand over his beard, gently stroking it as if pausing for thought. He would have been a man I would have called handsome had he not just called me stupid.

The silence felt like it had stretched for hours as he continued to hold my gaze. It was almost as if we were playing a game of chicken, seeing who would break first.

"Maybe I had my music too loud, that's probably why I didn't hear you," I spoke first, hoping to ease some of the tension filling the air between us.

"Seriously, your music was too loud? That's your excuse for evading a police officer? You've gotta be fucking kidding me," he muttered with disbelief in his tone as he shook his head at me.

"Bad word!" Theo proclaimed loudly. Finally, our staring contest ended as we both turned our attention to the back of the car. He clearly had yet to notice Theo in the backseat as I saw him jump slightly at the sound of his voice. The officer cleared his throat, adding more awkwardness to the already tense situation.

"So, you're driving around with your music too loud, a tail light out, and failing to pull over for the police with a child in the back?" he asked with a scowl, turning his attention back to me. *A tail light? Seriously?* He was causing all of this fuss over one of my lights being out?

"You're pulling me over for my tail light? That's it?" I could feel my calm tone starting to break into something more aggressive. "I don't know exactly what my son has to do with it and I've already explained to you I wasn't evading you. I pulled over the second I noticed you." There was a slight desperation to my voice. I didn't like what he was insinuating—he didn't know me and had no right to think I was putting my child in harm's way. Us being in this car, driving to this place, was me putting my child out of harm's way. This was supposed to be the start of new things, a fresh start. I hadn't even made it into our new town yet before getting pulled over by Officer Asshole.

"That's it? It's an offence to drive around with your lights out," he shot back. I felt like his eyes were starting to burn through me as he spoke.

"It's just one little thing, I don't see what all the fuss is for," I countered.

"It only takes one little thing, one little mistake, for something bad to happen. You have a child. I would have assumed you would be more responsible than that." His words made my stomach lurch and my fear quickly turned into anger running through my body.

How dare he.

There was no longer a hint of any calmness in my tone as I felt my voice begin to rise. "Listen here, Officer," my eyes scanned his badge, "Weatherston. I don't know who spat in your breakfast this morning, but I'm about this close," I held my hands up showing a small gap between my fingers to emphasise my point, "to calling your supervisor and filing a complaint. You have no right to accuse me of being a reckless mother. I would *never* put my child in harm's way." I felt myself shake with rage at his words.

There was a pause that felt like it went on forever. His face softened slightly as he looked at me. I could have sworn I even saw a small smile form on his lips as he stared.

"Go for it, sweetheart. You want my badge number, too?" He cocked his head at me, a smirk spreading across his lips. Yep, he was definitely smiling at me. I was so taken aback by his response and his smile I couldn't find the words to respond.

"Look, I'm feeling nice, today," he continued. The one-eighty he was taking threw me off. Why was he suddenly turning from Officer Stick-Up-His-Ass to Officer Sunshine?

"This is you feeling *nice*?" I interrupted, but he ignored me and continued.

"I'm going to write you up a warning. You need to get that light fixed ASAP, preferably today. If I catch you driving around again after today with it still out, you'll be seeing me again."

Whilst he may have been easy on the eyes, there was still no part of me that wanted to see him again anytime soon. I cursed him in my head, knowing he's just added another thing to my to-do list. One I'll have to get solved before I can get some sleep. The last thing I need is to run into Officer Sunshine tomorrow whilst I am trying to sort my life out.

He passed over the piece of paper with the warning. I could see he'd written his badge number and name at the top, as if to taunt me. He needn't have bothered–I wouldn't be forgetting about *Officer Weatherston* anytime soon. Why do all the hot ones have to be assholes?

Silence filled the air as our eyes found each other once more. What more was he expecting me to say? I still found myself trying to calm down from our initial interaction.

"You're welcome," he said, breaking the silence before turning around and sauntering back to his car.

I took a moment, just staring at the space he'd now vacated. I could feel my hands shaking with rage against the steering wheel. Had I made a mistake? I picked this place because it was supposed to offer us a better life. A safer life. If the people were like him, I guess we wouldn't be staying long.

I turned the vehicle back on, keeping the radio at a much lower volume this time. Turning around I could see his cruiser was still parked there. He was waiting for me to go first, I knew that much. I glanced quickly at Theo who was back on his iPad, seemingly unfazed by the interaction. After taking a deep breath, I pulled back on the road and headed towards town.

* * *

It didn't take long before I found myself in the heart of Rosehaven.

It looked just as beautiful as the pictures I had seen online.

I saw a sign for LW Auto Shop and pulled into it. I didn't have the time, knowledge, or patience to sort this issue myself. I'm certainly not risking seeing Officer Sunshine again, so I needed to get it sorted and off my list.

I was greeted by a man around my age as I got out of the car.

He smiled as he approached me. There was a warmth about him that instantly made the tension in my shoulders begin to lessen.

"Are you okay, ma'am?" His face softened as he took in what probably looked like a dishevelled state.

"Yeah, I was hoping you could help me. I was just pulled over by some ass-excuse for a cop. Apparently, my tail light is out and I need to get it fixed before I get a fine." I was rambling slightly; I probably shouldn't have led with the whole being pulled over thing. It didn't exactly give a great first impression of me, but I couldn't hide my anger. Who did he think he was, talking to me like that? I shook my head, trying to shake the image of his glare from my mind. "Is that something you could do for me? I'm only just moving into town, so I don't really have the means to do it." *I was definitely rambling now.*

"Of course. I can do it right now, if that's good with you? It'll only take a few minutes."

I felt a sense of relief at his response, one thing off the list. "Yes, please. Thank you, I really appreciate it. Do you mind if I get my son, Theo, out to watch? He has a bit of an obsession with cars."

He chuckled and smiled towards the back of my car. "Sure, let me just get my tools and I'll be back." As he walked away, I pulled Theo out of the backseat.

He may have only been three but he was obsessed with cars. I reckon if I had the right tools, he'd probably have been able to change the bulb for me himself. I watched as his eyes lit up at the sight of the man coming back with his tools.

"I'm Lucas, by the way." He smiled, extending out his hand as he walked back over. I took it and shook it softly. "Lottie, or Charlotte if I'm in trouble." This earned a small chuckle from Lucas. He reached his hand out, offering a high-five for Theo, which Theo gladly accepted.

"I guess that officer was probably calling you *Charlotte pretty* sternly just now." He smirked as he headed towards the back of the car. Theos' eyes didn't leave him for a moment, completely caught in a trance as he watched him work. "Can I ask what earned him the esteemed title of ass?"

"He insinuated I was a bad mother," I spoke frankly. I was still seething from his comment. Everything I was doing was for Theo, everything I *ever* did was for him. Everything I went through to make sure not a single hair on his head was hurt. "I'm not." My voice came out harsher than I meant.

"I don't think for one second you're a bad mother," he said, looking up. I took a deep breath, attempting to calm down. "What do you reckon, buddy? Have you got the best Mommy ever?" he asks, his attention now turned to Theo.

"The best one ever!" Theo mused excitedly. Lucas nodded in agreement before turning back to my car. I had to bite back my tears at the interaction. It was exactly what I needed to calm me down. I was doing a good job, no matter what anyone said. I needed to give myself more credit.

"Thank you. He seemed to find it funny when I said I was going to report him to his supervisor. Kindly wrote his badge number and name down for me. *Officer Weatherston,*" I added a slightly sarky tone of voice as I said his name.

"Hmm," was Lucas' short response. It suddenly occurred to me that the officer likely lived in the town and was potentially known to Lucas. Shit. I hoped I didn't just put my foot in it.

"Do you know him?"

"Yeah, I know him. It's a pretty small town." He turned his attention to me again. "If it makes you feel better, it's not hard to get on his bad side. I've definitely had a few run-ins with him. He's a bit of a grump."

He offered a reassuring smile before turning back to working on the car.

"That does make me feel better, thank you." I guess Officer Sunshine made a habit of ruining other people's days, too.

There were a few moments of silence whilst Lucas finished working. "All done." He rose to his feet to face me.

"Amazing, what do I owe you?" I asked, reaching for my purse in the car. I was really hoping the number he would respond with would be small.

"Nothing, it's on the house." He shot me a small smile. "And before you try to argue, I'm not changing my mind–it took me five minutes. I'm sorry you had a bad morning; I hope you don't think everyone in this town is like Officer Weatherston."

Up until that point, I *was* worried that everyone would be like him. I was worried I had just moved from one bad situation to another. I was grateful for the kindness Lucas was showed me. "I don't think that now." I couldn't help but blush slightly. "Thank you, but you really don't have to."

He held his hand up as if to remind me that he said not to argue. "It's my pleasure. If you're moving into town, I'm sure I'll see you around. Don't forget about me if you have any car trouble," he added with a wink.

"You'll be the first person I call." I laughed as I started to load Theo back into the car.

"If you need anything, it doesn't necessarily have to be car trouble, even with the move, here is my card." He reached into his pocket and handed me a card which I slid straight into my bag without looking. He was just being friendly; I wasn't about to start taking advantage of his kindness by asking him for help. "Or if the little dude just wants to come watch us work on cars, he's always welcome."

I thanked him again before we said our goodbyes and I returned once more to my car. Finally, we made our way to the hotel. After checking in, we collapsed straight onto the beds. It had been a long, first day in Rosehaven.

Six

Elijah

I had walked over to that car with so much anger in my body, I thought I was going to explode. However, I came away feeling a complete mixture of emotions as I sat myself back down in the driver's seat.

As much as I didn't want to admit it, I may have allowed my emotions to dominate that situation more than I had liked. I had expected the driver to be some stupid, young guy thinking he was above the law. The last thing I had expected was someone like *her*.

Charlotte Miller.

Her name dangled in the air as I stared out the front of my car. I rubbed my hands over my face as I watched her car pull away from me.

I felt slightly guilty for being hard on her, but she was being reckless, stupid. I felt the annoyance find its way back to the forefront of my emotions.

There was something about her though that made me change my mind. My instincts were telling me that she was vulnerable, that something was amiss with the whole situation. There was something in her eyes that made the anger disappear and concern take precedent.

Truthfully, I was a little distracted by her.

I'd almost forgotten why I pulled her over in the first place. It wasn't very often people stood up to me like that, especially not people who looked like her. Her defensiveness felt over the top to me, as if I had really hit a nerve with my comments. I couldn't place my finger on why the interaction bothered me so much. I'm missing something.

The situation could have been so different if I hadn't pulled her over, though. If she had continued on driving recklessly instead of me pulling her over, I could have been pulling her body out of the car. The images that came with that thought made my stomach turn. A quiet scream just above a whisper filled my ears. I quickly shook the thoughts and noises away.

Maybe I was harsh on her, but she needed it. Sometimes people just need tough love in order to see their errors. She won't be doing that again, that was for sure. I tried to convince myself I was justified in my response to the situation, although I still had that niggling feeling. It doesn't matter, I'd let her off with a warning, I'd shown her kindness. Other officers probably would have fined her on the spot.

I probably *should* have fined her, but I couldn't bring myself to do it. I don't think I would have been able to look her in the eye as I handed her the fine. She looked vulnerable and honestly exhausted. I was tough, but I wasn't a monster; especially not with a little boy in the back.

The last few hours of my shift passed through without

incident. Nobody spoke to me about the events of the day when I was clocking out, so it was a fair assumption that she hadn't reported me. Not yet, anyway. Whilst I felt justified in my response, that didn't necessarily mean my boss would.

Heading back home, I'd hoped my brother would be there ready for our dinner when I got back, but the house was quiet. As if reading my thoughts, my phone buzzed in my pocket.

L: Running late, meet you at Blake's in an hour.

I guess I should have predicted that.

At least he was still coming. I wouldn't have put it past him to completely blow me off. I took my time showering off the stress of the day before getting ready for dinner. I stared at myself in the mirror, trying to figure out how to cheer myself up. I wasn't exactly going to be great dinner company if I couldn't rid myself of this foul mood. I struggled to get the day off my mind, to get *her* off my mind. I felt some guilt try to creep its way in, but I shut it down quickly before making my way out the door.

Blake's was mostly quiet and I was grateful for that. I gave a polite nod to a few people I knew as I walked over to the booth my brother was seated at near the back.

"Nice of you to finally join, Eli," he said, a smug grin covering his face. He was still in his work clothes; I was hoping he'd at least have the decency to change before meeting me.

"Bit rich coming from the man in dirty overalls, don't you think, Lucas?" I countered, placing myself down across from him.

"I'll have you know the dirty overalls look is quite popular with women. I feel it's starting to rival the love for a man in uniform." He chuckled as he put down the menu. "How was your day?"

I answered him with a grunt, which earned me a raised eyebrow from him, encouraging me to go on. "I was called to a couple of teenagers robbing Lucky's this morning. I was chasing one of them down." I paused to thank the waitress for the water she brought over. "My leg cramped up and he got away." The frustration rolled off my tongue as I spoke.

I felt Lucas' eyes on me for a moment before he spoke. We'd become closer in recent years after I let him move into my house. He wanted some independence from our mother, but wasn't quite able to afford his own space whilst he was building his business. I'd already bought my house by then and was happy to have him there. As annoying as he was, he brought a lightness to the space where the darkness had begun to consume it.

The silence of the house before he moved in had bothered me more than I cared to admit. Selfishly, I didn't want him to move out. I didn't want to have to live alone again.

"It happens som—"

"It shouldn't happen," I interrupted him before he could finish. "I should have caught them."

"You don't have to be perfect all the time, Elijah. Sometimes these things are going to happen. You can't exactly predict that you're going to get cramp. It isn't your fault."

Except it was my fault, but I didn't bother to argue his point. If I hadn't run so far this morning, I may not have gotten a cramp in my leg. But to explain that would mean explaining why I ran so far in the first place. I wasn't about to talk about that.

Sensing my unwillingness to discuss it further, he continued,

"What about the rest of your shift?"

"Uneventful," I lied. This afternoon was yet another thing I didn't particularly want to discuss right now. I didn't really want to talk about her.

"How are things in the car fixing world?" I asked in an attempt to deflect the conversation away from me.

"This morning was pretty uneventful, however something interesting did happen this afternoon." He paused his story as one of the waitresses approached and took our order. Once she had gone, he continued.

"I had a walk-in. Now I normally turn away walk-ins that late in the day, but she was gorgeous. That and I'm a softie." He smirked, turning to me. "Apparently some ass of a cop had pulled her over and was chewing her out about her tail light."

Son of a bitch.

My stomach dropped at his words. *Charlotte Miller.* I could feel his smirk even though I wasn't looking at him. I knew he had already made the connection. I didn't even think about the fact she would go to Lucas' shop. I guess it makes sense, considering I told her to sort it today. When I didn't respond, Lucas continued.

"Officer Weatherston, she told me. Real nasty guy who said some horrible things to her." He paused. "Was there a particular reason you decided to be mean towards this beautiful woman?"

"She didn't pull over when I first started blaring sirens at her–it took her ages to even clock me. She was driving recklessly; I wasn't mean, just giving her some tough love," I countered .

"She still looked pissed when she showed up to my shop. Said you implied she was a bad mother." He sighed.

"What were you thinking, Eli?"

I mentally noted that it was about a twenty-minute drive from where I pulled her over to Lucas' shop. I couldn't help but enjoy the fact that she was still thinking about our interaction when she got there, even if she was pissed.

"I didn't say she was a bad mother, I simply said I would have expected someone with a child to be more responsible. She was being reckless!" My voice raised slightly on the last sentence.

"Were you angry at what she was doing or were you just pissed off that those two teenagers got away this morning, then took it out on the next person you came across?"

I would never admit this to him, but there was a high chance he was right. It irritated me how well my brother knew me.

"What did she say when she found out you were the brother of the asshole cop that pulled her over?"

"Oh god, I did not tell Lottie you were my brother. She was furious with you."

"*Lottie?*" I asked incredulously, annoyance laced in my voice. "You're on a nickname basis now, are you?"

"Don't blow a gasket, that's how she introduced herself to me. I kept it purely on a first name basis. I was not going to kill my shot with an attractive woman by telling her I was related to *you*," he teased, nudging me.

I couldn't help but feel a bitter taste in my mouth listening to his words, talking about having a shot with her. I quickly let it go and changed the subject. It wasn't worth the argument. But I couldn't help but feel slightly disappointed that her tail light was fixed. I had wondered if our paths would cross again.

Seven

Charlotte

We spent the rest of the day relaxing in the hotel room.

I was both physically and emotionally exhausted.

It was still early when I woke up. Despite having some of the best sleep I'd had in months, my brain was now wide awake. I decided to take the opportunity to have a shower and wake myself up for the day ahead. After the shower I looked at my phone. I hadn't dared look at it until now.

Adam: Where the hell are you?

Adam: Stop messing around and get your ass back here. Now.

I felt myself tense at the messages even though I knew they were coming. There must have been over twenty sent in the last day alone. All of them were laced with anger and made me feel terrified. Should we have left? Did I just put us in more danger? As I scrolled through the messages, I felt my resolve harden. We couldn't have stayed another second.

Moving to Rosehaven had been a slightly last-ditch effort. Luckily for me, I had always been a slightly spontaneous person so I knew we would adapt. I couldn't handle people who were too meticulous about everything they did–not everything needed to be taken so seriously. That being said, whilst I was spontaneous, I wasn't naïve. I had a bit of a thing about making lists. As long as I wrote everything down, I would be fine. I was a little too scatty otherwise.

As well as getting things done, I was looking forward to exploring more of this town. I spent time researching and it just looked so beautiful.

It had also been rated one of the safest towns to live in by some small magazine. I had never heard of it before until the other night and that's also part of the reason I chose it. He would never think to look for us here.

After getting both of us ready and fed at the hotel, we headed out towards a local park I found nearby. The first two things on my list were to find us a place to rent and to find a job. I knew I would need to figure out childcare arrangements as well, but one step at a time. Theo ran excitedly off to play with the other kids the second we entered the play area. He had always been extremely extroverted and had no trouble going up to complete strangers and inserting himself into their games and conversations. It always made me smile to watch him playing. His face was animated as they were all setting the scene for whatever imaginary scenario they were in. He may look like his dad, but their personalities were polar opposites and I was grateful for that. I wouldn't change my kind, inquisitive boy for anything.

I settled myself to a bench on the side so I could still keep him in my line of sight. I wished I had grabbed another coffee to go when we left the hotel as I pulled out my phone to look at property listings. I had about enough saved for the deposit and first month's rent, but I really needed to find a job before we moved somewhere. I was so engrossed in sending off my enquires I hadn't noticed I was no longer alone on the bench.

"Is that your son in the blue?" The voice made me jump slightly as I turned to the woman who was now beside me. I guess I was feeling a bit on edge still. She looked vaguely familiar, but I couldn't place it. I don't think I've met her before, but I can't shake the feeling she looks like someone I know. My eyes moved over to Theo who was now playing with a young blonde girl on the slide.

"Yeah, that's my son, Theo. Is that your daughter with him?" I put my phone in my pocket before turning my attention to her.

"It is, her name's Violet. She's usually very shy, but she seems to be in her element with Theo." She had a slight chuckle in her voice as she spoke.

"Theo can sort of bring that out of people sometimes. He basically goes about the world thinking everyone is his best friend and wants to chat to him." I smiled softly. "Some people are too polite to tell him to get lost." *Adam wasn't.* On the rare occasions we went out as a family, he always got annoyed by Theo. He hated having to endure small talk with strangers and Theo was an expert at doing just that. I was the one who was punished when we got home, told how I needed to rein *our* son in. That *I* wasn't raising him correctly. No matter how angry he got, I never tried to change anything about Theo's nature. I wasn't going to lessen his sparkle.

She laughed at my comment and I was brought back to the present. Her eyes left the kids and turned to me. "I think Violet needs someone like that, to be honest. She always seems to be standing just outside the group." She held out her hand to me. "I'm Alice, by the way."

I took her hand, offering her a smile.

"I'm Charlotte, although most people call me Lottie."

"Lottie," she echoed as she matched my smile.

"Are you visiting someone in town? I don't think I've seen you guys around before."

"Just moved here, actually. We only arrived yesterday." There was something comforting about Alice's presence that I couldn't quite place. I relaxed myself into the bench as I continued, "I've been utilising the time Theo's been playing to look at listings of places to live. Job hunting is next."

"Is it just the two of you?" she asked. I could hear the slight hesitation in her voice as she asked. I guess I should get used to people asking that question, although I'd be lying if I said it didn't sting a little.

"Yeah, it's just us two now." I tried to hide the slight shake in my voice as I answered.

"It's just Violet and I, too. Well, her dad and I are still married, but we're starting the divorce process soon. He lives out in the city."

"Oh, I'm sorry." I guess I was lucky that Adam and I never married. It makes it a lot less messy to cut ties.

"I'm not." There was a determination in her voice as she replied.

"Sometimes things are better on your own, you know?" I

did know, I knew exactly what she meant. I knew it more than I cared to admit at this moment.

We talked a while longer whilst the kids continued playing. Alice told me that she ran a book store in the town and lived with her mother just on the outside of town. She moved back in when she separated from her husband. She told me all about how her ma dotes on Violet. I kept the conversation light on my side. I told her how I fell pregnant with Theo in college and had been a stay-at-home mother since he was born. I used to waitress at a diner in college, which is where I met Adam. After a while the kids ran up and Theo was complaining that he was hungry.

"I was planning on taking Violet for lunch at the café if you want to join?" Alice asked.

"Yes!" Theo beat me to answering, making us laugh. "We'd love to," I chimed in and I meant it. After the less than warm welcome I got when I entered town yesterday, it was nice to find a friend. And I really needed a friend right now.

Caffeine Central was buzzing from the start of the lunch rush when we arrived. Sending the kids off to claim us a table, we waited at the counter to order. Our eyes both fell to the help wanted sign on the desk.

"Are you still looking for someone for that position, Jane?" Alice asked as she stepped up to the front.

"Yeah, I can't seem to find anyone. I was just talking about it with your brother yesterday, actually. Asked him to keep an eye out for me." She smiled. "You know anyone looking?"

"My friend Lottie is looking, actually," she said, pointing to me.

"Oh, yeah. I just moved here yesterday. I was actually planning on asking around to see who was hiring later today."

I couldn't help but smile when Alice referred to me as a friend. It was comforting to know she was looking out for me.

"Really?" Jane asked, turning her full attention to me. "Do you have any experience?"

"I waitressed my way through college before I had Theo," I said, pointing over to where the kids were sitting. "I've been a stay-at-home since I had him, though."

"Sounds good to me. How would you feel about doing a trial shift and seeing how we go from there?" I had to try to keep my face from giving too much of my shock as to how easy that had been. If I could do a good trial shift, that would be the first thing on my list ticked off, not to mention a huge weight off of my shoulders. I guess having Alice to vouch for me helped massively, even though she hardly knew me, either.

"That would be great!"

I answered before I suddenly remembered Theo. "Oh, shoot. I would just need to sort some childcare out for Theo. I was planning on looking at day cares later, too." I suddenly felt anxious; I didn't want to blow the opportunity. I guess I didn't quite think about the logistics of being on my own.

"My friend runs a day care down the road. Violet goes there when Ma and I are both working. I can give her a call and help you get Theo set up there?" Alice offers.

It's official, Alice is quite literally my guardian angel. I am convinced at any second I'm going to wake up and none of this would be real. We spoke to Jane more as she took our order, and providing Theo gets set up okay, I have my trial shift tomorrow afternoon. I was falling more and more in love with the town and its people by the minute. Yesterday's drama was becoming a distant memory, just a small blip on our timeline. Everything was going to be okay; we were going to be happy here. I could feel it.

Eight

Elijah

I had Thursday off so I spent my morning at the gym. After yesterday's disaster chasing those two boys, I was all fired up. I needed to be stronger, more agile. They may have gotten the best of me yesterday, but it wouldn't happen again. I wouldn't allow it. I also couldn't shake last night's conversation with Lucas. I've never claimed to be the friendliest guy in town, but I didn't make a habit of scolding women over tail lights. I had allowed my anger from the morning to seep through to my work. I imagine she spent most of her evening complaining about it to her husband and he'd probably be knocking down my door soon enough. I utilised this anger to push through another few reps before making my way home.

Even after a workout, shower, and lunch, I still found myself tense as I pondered my next move. My eyes wandered over to the piano in the corner.

Lucas wouldn't be home for a while yet; he knew I played,

but I didn't like anyone watching me whilst I did. I didn't exactly play to perform, I played to relieve tension.

When I was in high school, I used to find myself feeling panicky or angry most days.

I wasn't coping well, but I did my best to hide the fact. I would go and sit in a quiet classroom, closing my eyes, wishing the feelings away. Eventually, I would calm down enough to go back to class, but the anxious feeling never really left me.

One day I had a particularly bad turn. I felt like my heart was going to rip straight out of my chest. I could feel it pounding over and over as I gasped for air. No matter what I did, I felt like I couldn't breathe, like I had no control over my body. I was slumped down in a quiet corridor when Mr. Lawson found me. He sat with me until I calmed down and had my breathing under control before leading me into the music room. It was quite well known to everyone in the school what happened in our family, but he never asked about it. He never made me talk about any of it.

Instead, he taught me to play piano. He would make time for me every day to come and play. He even eventually gave me a key to a practice room so I could have access to a piano whenever I needed it. When I played it made me forget about everything that was going on. The tightness in my chest would lessen and my mind would focus on nothing else but the music. Playing would take me out of my head and into a completely new world where I was at peace.

I moved away from my kitchen table and started playing. As my fingers ran along the keys, I felt the tension releasing from my shoulders. I closed my eyes briefly on the part I knew by heart and took a deep breath. I would play until I felt better, this was one of the only things I did for me. It wasn't a secret so much as I didn't actively relay this information to anyone outside of my family. Even then, I didn't explain to them how much I needed to play. How playing was the only time I felt truly calm and happy.

A while later a slamming of the front door interrupted my playing as I took my hands off the keys.

"Don't stop on my account," Lucas said as he walked into the room. I didn't like to play to an audience, this was just for me.

"I was about to stop anyway; we need to head over to Ma's for dinner soon," I said as I shut the top and started to move away.

"Oh yes, how could I forget Thursday night dinner!" He chuckled, putting his bag down.

"Yep, Thursday night dinner," I echoed.

It was my Ma's enforced tradition that we made time for dinner every Thursday as much as possible.

Occasionally I was on a night shift and missed it, but when I could be I was there. She would never admit it, but I know my mother has been lonely in recent years. It was slightly better now my sister was back living with her, but I know it's been hard on her. She spent most of her time when we were growing up fussing over all of us. It was our time to take care of her now. It was part of my job.

I drove us over a little while later, figuring Lucas needed a beer more than I did after his day working. As usual, we were greeted by my ma's warm embrace the second we walked through the door.

It felt like each time she held on a little longer and tighter than the last.

"Uncle Eli!" The sound of my niece's footsteps came charging through the house.

"You've been behaving yourself, Vi?" I asked as I picked her up. "You know I will take you down to the station if you haven't." She laughed as she wrapped her arms around my neck.

"Obviously, I'm always good." She wasn't far off. I might be biased, but she is one of the sweetest little girls. "I made a new best friend today."

"That she did," my sister, Alice, said, coming out of the kitchen. "She spent all morning playing with this little boy."

"*A boy?*" Lucas chimed in, almost at the same time as I said, "Absolutely not." which prompted a laugh from both my mother and Alice.

"Boys, she's *four*. We also should be happy that she made a friend!" Alice said, her tone of voice stern. Alice was always worrying about how shy Violet was.

It wouldn't be much longer before she was starting school. Alice was worried she wouldn't be able to make friends. I had always been a shy kid like Violet. I knew it was important for her to be able to make friends and be more outgoing. I wanted better from my niece than what I had.

"You're right, we're proud of you." I tickled her as I put her back down so she could greet Lucas.

"God help her when she does actually start dating with you two around." Alice chuckled, patting my arm as she headed back to the living room.

"God help *them*," Ma replied, following her.

She wasn't wrong–Violet had two protective uncles to watch out for her. Any future romantic interests would be lucky if we let them within two feet of her.

In a similar way that Thursday dinners became a habit, so was us sitting in the same chair at the table as we did when we were little. We all sat down as my mother brought out one of her famous chicken pot pies. My ma and the café were the only reasons I was eating well.

I couldn't help but find my eyes wandering to my dad's empty seat at the end of the table.

Every Thursday it was empty, it had been for fifteen years. Nobody ever sat there, not even guests. It felt like it was just waiting there for him, that one day I would come to Thursday dinner and he would be sat there. It was never going to happen, though. The only thing that chair was doing was collecting dust. Alice must have caught me looking as I felt her hand softly touch mine. We didn't talk about it much anymore. No matter how much time passed, it was still too painful for me.

Sometimes when any of us were hitting milestones or when I looked at Violet, I felt a pang in my chest. He would have doted on her just like my mother does, but he never got to meet her. He never got to sit around this table, listening to her tell her bizarre stories whilst the rest of us soaked in her every word like she was reciting some Shakespearean masterpiece. We were all quite soft on her, really, but she felt like this flicker of light in the darkness that hung over this family.

At Alice's touch I turned my attention away from dad's chair. Taking a deep breath, I try to push those thoughts from my mind. Part of me wishes Ma would move houses so we weren't haunted by it, but part of me never wanted to let it go. I turned my attention back to my family as they spoke, soaking in every word, every moment we had together.

Nine

Charlotte

After lunch with Alice, we parted ways as I headed down to the day care to get Theo registered. Alice had pulled a favour in with her friend so I was able to do my trial shift the next afternoon. I spent the rest of the afternoon sending off more enquires for potential places to live. For now, the hotel room felt like a fun little holiday, but I was aware that fun would soon run out. We viewed a few of the properties the next morning before my shift. There was only one that looked promising enough for us to live within my price range. I tried to ignore the negative feelings rising up as I put in the application. If it didn't work out there would be more. Besides, I was going to ace this trial shift and everything would find its own way of working out. If I allowed myself to think it was going to go badly, then it would. I needed to remain positive.

I recognised that attitude as being very much like my

grandma Lily. She was the one who engrained it in me to stay positive. I had lost my way with that recently, but I was determined to bring that side back out. Theo needed me to be that mother for him as much as I needed to be it for myself.

It dawned on me as I took Theo to day care the next day that I had never left him anywhere like this before. Occasionally over the years, Adam's parents or a neighbour had watched him whilst we were out, but not complete strangers. Not in this kind of environment. I knew he was confident enough to excel in the situation, but it did nothing to stop my anxiety. I watched as he ran off, making a beeline straight for Violet who was drawing in the corner. One of the carers tried to reassure me he would be okay. I guess I wasn't doing a good job at hiding my nerves. It did nothing to calm the guilt that was rising up inside of me.

Being a stay-at-home mother was never in my plans. Being a mother at all hadn't really been in my sights, either. Adam and I weren't exactly the most careful, so I guess I shouldn't have been that surprised to get pregnant in college. He was a little bit older than me and something about that captivated me. Adam was always so charming when we first got together. His words always seemed to put me exactly where he needed me to be. When they found out I was pregnant, my parents refused to talk to me. They've never even met Theo. Adam simply brushed it off. He told me he was the only person I needed anyway, so it didn't matter that my parents weren't going to be around. I believed him at the time, although it hurt not to have my mother around on the harder days of pregnancy and parenting.

Theodore was my grandpa's name, but everyone called him Theo. I wanted to honour him in some way for everything he'd done for me. Adam didn't put up much of a fight with the name as long as Theo had his surname, Thompson. The name Theodore means divine gift or god's gift. It felt fitting for my grandpa and it fit Theo, too. He may have been unexpected, but he was a gift to me. One I often wasn't sure I deserved.

After he was born, Adam insisted I be a stay-at-home mom. He earned enough money to support us both and hated the idea of me being away from the house. I never bothered arguing with him, but I often wonder now if me being at home was less about Theo and more about his desire for control. If I wasn't earning my own pay check and going out every day, I was easier for him to isolate, easier to manipulate. I had managed to sell some of my grandma's jewellery before Theo and I left. It was the only way to get any money to leave.

I shook the thoughts of Adam from my head. I didn't have time to dwell on that, I needed to focus on my trial shift. The money from the bits I sold would only go so far, I could really do with securing this job.

Jane gave me a similar, warm greeting as she had done the previous day. There was something motherly about her and it warmed my heart. It was a void that I often forgot I had in my life. She seemed to fill the role so naturally as she took the time to take me through how everything worked. After a couple hours it felt like no time had passed since my waitressing days. The people of Rosehaven were all so kind, greeting me like they would an old friend. I soon found my rhythm serving the patrons of Caffeine Central.

"Lottie!" The sound of a girl's voice caused me to turn my head towards the door. Violet bounded up to the counter, smiling at me. I looked behind her expecting to see Alice—she had texted me *good luck* earlier, saying she would probably stop by for a coffee later. To my surprise, Violet was followed in by Lucas.

"Oh, hi," I said, not doing a very good job of hiding my surprise of seeing him. Luckily, he looked just as confused as I was.

"Hey, fancy seeing you here. How do you know Violet?" he added with a soft smile.

"I bumped into Alice and Violet in the park yesterday with my son. They ended up spending most of the day together." I smiled back. "Sorry, I didn't realise you were her dad."

"Oh, no," he responded almost too quickly with a wave of his hand. "I'm her uncle, Alice is my sister. She got delayed at work so asked me to pick up Violet from day care and bring her over to the shop. Figured we'd sneak a little takeaway hot chocolate and treat on our way over."

I was slightly relieved to find out he wasn't Violet's dad. Alice didn't exactly speak too fondly about her ex. Lucas seemed like a nice guy, it would have been disappointing to find out he was one of the bad ones.

"Ah, does that mean Theo is the new best friend you were going on about?" he asked Violet. "She was going on and on last night about her new best friend she made. I never caught the name of him."

"Oh, yeah. They were like ducks in the water together."

"Well, I can't say I was overly happy that she had spent all day hanging out with a boy. Although, I feel better knowing it was Theo." Violet was hiding shyly behind his leg, clearly not enjoying being the centre of the conversation.

"She's four," I reassured with a chuckle.

"That's *exactly* what Alice said."

We chatted for a while longer whilst I made their drinks

and packed up their treats. Lucas asked if I had been pulled over again since he last saw me, to which I informed him luckily, I had not. We talked about the café, how I got the trial shift, and about Theo and Violet's budding friendship. Once I had finished putting everything together, I passed it over the counter towards them, earning a soft thank you from Violet.

"Well, that was incredible service, wasn't it, Vi? Couldn't ask for better staff to be served by," Lucas said purposely loud, stretching his gaze towards Jane who was working behind me. He earned a laugh from her. "It was nice seeing you, I'm sure we will run into each other again," he said. We said our goodbyes and they headed back out of the café.

The café went through a period of quiet as Jane approached me.

"So, how do we feel about making this position more permanent?" she asked. I felt my heart start to jump in my chest.

"Really, you mean it?" I needed someone to pinch me.

"Of course. You haven't missed a beat the whole shift, we'd be lucky to have you." We spent some time hashing out the details and expectations whilst it was quiet. Theo was already signed up for day care, so I just needed to arrange it around my shifts. After we had organised everything, I was back on the counter. I only had half an hour left before I could go pick him up. I would be lying if I said I wasn't missing him, but the café was busy so it kept my mind off of it.

The bell on the door jingled as it opened and I found my head snapping up to see who was entering. I tried my best to keep my breath steady as my gaze found theirs.

"Well, if it isn't Officer Sunshine," I beamed teasingly at him. "Steal any candy from babies today?"

Ten

Elijah

I felt like the wind had been knocked out of me as my eyes found their way to the source of the voice.

It was her. She was here working in the café. I tried to ignore the *Officer Sunshine* comment, but I couldn't help but feel a tinge of annoyance at the nickname. She was goading me, trying to get a reaction. I was not in the mood for her antics.

There were a few moments of silence as we seemed to stare at each other in a state of shock. I allowed my eyes to wander down her body briefly. Having only seen part of her in the car, I took a moment to take the rest of her in. I'm not sure how long my eyes had been lingering before Jane broke through the silence.

"You two know each other?" she questioned, her eyes darting between the two of us. Charlotte cleared her throat awkwardly before she spoke.

"I got pulled over by Officer Weatherston on my way into town." She paused, turning to frown at me. "My tail light was out," she added.

"Oh! Did you help her fit a new bulb? He once helped me fix mine when it was out. Elijah's always so helpful," Jane beamed.

Charlotte snorted, as if the idea of me being helpful was a hilarious concept to her. I would be lying if I said that didn't sting a bit, but it was probably deserved given our interaction.

"Oh no, I sorted it elsewhere," she answered as Jane moved off to clear some tables. "So, you don't have to worry about pulling me over again," she added for my benefit, turning her attention back to me.

"Well, I am glad to hear it. Although, I'm still waiting to hear about your complaint from my supervisor or did you just go home and rant about it to your husband?" I asked with a raised brow.

"I didn't make a complaint and I don't have a husband, so no ranting about it at home, either. Although, I did have some choice words for you in my diary." I laughed almost a little too loud at that.

"I don't know whether to tease you about still writing a diary or be honoured that I was important enough to be in it." The egotistical part of me enjoyed imagining her writing about me in the diary; her features all scrunched up as her pen scribbled obscenities about me on the pages. Our interaction forever entrapped in the pages. I also couldn't help but enjoy hearing her say there was no husband. I had assumed, given the child in the back of the car.

A smile formed my lips as I watched her blush a little.

"You should try writing in a diary sometime, might help with your anger issues." There was a hint of tension in her voice as she bit back.

"You know, I find people pulling over when I ask them to helps massively with my anger issues." I couldn't help but rise to her remark.

"Are you going to order a coffee or do you just enjoy wasting my time?" Truthfully, I did quite enjoy wasting her time.

"Don't let Jane hear you talking to customers that way," I teased. "A nice large coffee to go, *please*," I said, overemphasising the last word, pulling some cash out of my wallet. I had a night shift tonight so I definitely needed the caffeine.

"So, when did you start working here?" I asked, hoping to extend some kind of an olive branch following our previous, tense interaction.

"Today was my trial shift, although Jane has just signed me on as an official employee," she said, turning away from me to make my coffee. It gave me an excuse to look at her again. Her long, auburn hair flowed down to her sides. I caught myself staring at the way her jeans hugged her hips. In my rage the other day, I had clocked that she was pretty, but I hadn't quite appreciated just how beautiful she was. She turned back to me and I realised I needed to break my gaze before she caught me.

"Well, I guess we will be seeing a lot more of each other," I quipped, taking the coffee from her.

"Lucky me, I can't wait," she responded sarcastically. Before I could counter back, the bell of the door caught both of our attention.

Officer Taylor and Lawrence strolling in, I had hoped to avoid them before the start of the shift.

"Well, unless Jane has gotten younger and more beautiful, I would say we have a fresh face in here," Officer Taylor said as he walked over. I tensed, ready to jump to Charlotte's defence, but to my surprise, his words were met with a giggle from her. Was she being polite or did she actually find this asshole funny? Her laugh did nothing but make my body even tenser than before.

"I'm Lottie," she said, smiling over to them. I'll let Lucas off; she did introduce herself that way.

"I'm Daniel, or Danny, if you'd prefer, and this is Andy," he said, pointing to Officer Lawrence.

"Well, it's nice to meet you both. What can I get for you?" My eyes narrowed on Daniel as she took their orders. I watched as his eyes followed her around with a smug look on his face. I could feel the anger rising up inside of me. The irony of the fact I had been looking at her too was not lost on me, but this was different. Daniel and Andy were not good people and they didn't deserve to get to look at her like that. I wanted to keep her safe and far away from assholes like them. I was finished being served, but my feet didn't move. I watched and listened as they asked her questions about when she started working here and where she moved from.

"So, what's a pretty girl like you doing moving to a place like Rosehaven?" Daniel asked. I saw her blush slightly at his words and I tensed just a little more. If I tensed any more, I was sure I was going to combust.

"Just getting a fresh start for my son and I. I heard this place had a pretty low crime rate. Must mean you guys have a pretty good police force, eh?" she added with a wink.

"For sure. We have some bad guys around, but don't worry; keeping you safe just became my top priority," Daniel replied with a smirk.

I gripped my coffee cup so tight it exploded in my hand,

sending the burning liquid straight down my arm. Charlotte gasped before running around to my side of the counter. I could feel all eyes suddenly on me, but the anxiety of that did nothing to lessen the pain from the burn. Before I could react, Charlotte grabbed my other arm, adding a slight bolt of electricity to my burning pain. She dragged me behind the counter towards the sink, taking my wrist gently in her other hand she placed it under the cold tap.

"Are you okay?" she asked softly, our faces mere inches from each other.

"I'm fine." My voice was gruff. My pride wanted to snatch my hand away from her, but I left it there. I allowed her to take complete control of my arm as she rinsed it off. She stood there with me for a while as I felt the burning sensation starting to lessen. Jane had taken over Daniel and Andy's orders and I turned my head slightly, watching them walk away. I took a small pleasure in having interrupted their attempts to flirt with Charlotte.

"Let me make you another coffee. Keep your hand under there for a bit longer," she said as she removed her hand and walked away to the coffee machine. My eyes lingered on the spot where her hand had been. A slight empty feeling took over me in the absence of her touch.

I removed my hand from the cold water. There was still a slight pain in my arm, but the wound to my ego was a lot worse. I had allowed my anger to bubble over again. I couldn't help but feel anxious watching Danny and Charlotte interact. I couldn't place why, but the thought of it made me feel sick. This was *not* how I wanted to start my night shift. Suddenly I felt myself longing for my piano. To feel the keys under my fingers and allow the calm to wash over me. I would be able to play after my shift, I would have to hold out till then.

"Are you sure you're okay?" Charlotte asked as she brought over a replacement coffee.

"Yeah, I'm good. Sorry about the mess." My eyes moved over to the spot where I had dropped my coffee. Jane had already been round and cleared it up. I reached my hand in my pocket to get some more cash out.

"Don't worry about that," Charlotte said, holding her hand out to stop me. "I've already squared it with Jane." She took a step closer as she spoke.

"Thank you. I better get to work," I said, clearing my throat as I took a step back.

"Of course. You better get to it—the citizens of Rosehaven are desperate for Officer Sunshine to spread his joy around," she teased, chuckling as she headed back behind the counter.

I had a feeling I would be drinking even more coffee now than I already did.

Eleven

Charlotte

The last thirty minutes of my shift definitely took a weird turn.

Jane had told me that most of their business was police officers from the station, so I made sure to be polite when the officers came in. They were harmless enough aside from the flirting. I couldn't help but be slightly flattered by it. I've been with Adam so long, it had been a while since I'd been paid that kind of attention. Besides, I could do with the tip money.

I was happy to play along, despite not being overly enthusiastic about dating anytime soon. Maybe one of them would change my mind. There was something about Officer Weatherston, who I now know is called Elijah, that really gets under my skin. He always seems to have some snarky remark for me. Although, I couldn't help but feel slightly sorry for him when he spilled his coffee on himself. I instantly felt this need to take care of him. There was a certain softness that seemed to let its way into him when I was helping him.

While he normally seemed to be snarky or give sarcastic comments, it was nice to see a hint of vulnerability beneath the surface.

After all of that excitement, I was glad my shift was over and I could head over to pick up Theo. I pulled out my phone and started going through my notifications. I deleted the texts from Adam without bothering to read them; I didn't want to know what he had to say. I spied an email from the realtor and found myself stopping dead in my tracks.

My application has been accepted for the apartment.

It was already empty; we could pick up the keys whenever we were ready. I let out an involuntary squeal as I finished reading the email. The apartment was small and not exactly our forever home, but it was a start. It was a way to begin our fresh start and get out of the hotel. It felt like for once, things were finally starting to go our way. I fired off a quick email back, asking if I could collect the keys tomorrow, hoping they would be open on a Saturday. I would have to sort out some furniture and other bits before we could actually move in, but I was excited to at least have the keys.

I continued to go through my notifications as I set about walking again and saw a text from Alice.

Alice: Sorry I didn't get a chance to come see you, got a big order come through late in the day. Lucas said you were doing great, though! Want to go get dinner with the kiddos tonight to celebrate?

I really shouldn't have been that surprised that Lucas and Alice were siblings. They both had this supportive nature about them, you really got the feeling that they were in your corner. I had sensed a familiarity when I first met Alice and it must have been their similar nature. Both of them had been nothing but kind to Theo and I since we came into town and I was grateful for them. I fired her back a text to arrange the time and place before walking into the day care to get Theo. We had an hour or so before we arranged to see Alice and Violet, so we walked back to the hotel to get showered and ready. I spent the whole walk asking Theo to tell me everything. He seemed so happy and it put my heart at ease. This was going to become our new normal. I was anxious he would struggle to adjust, but he seemed more settled than I'd ever seen him.

Alice had suggested that we meet at a place called Blake's Diner, she said it was a fond favourite of her family. It was an old eighties style diner lined with booths and various decorations from the time period. Alice and Violet were already there when we arrived and the kids quickly started colouring.

"How did it go?" Alice asked excitedly as I sat down.

"Really good, Jane offered me the job!" I couldn't hide my own excitement in my response.

I felt like I could finally breathe and I was not afraid to celebrate that.

"That's amazing, Lottie!" Her smile was genuine as she turned to me. "Lucas and Violet gave rave reviews about your hot chocolate to me." Violet briefly turned away from her drawing to give me a thumbs up.

"The highest of compliments," I said with a laugh. "I didn't realise you and Lucas were related. What a small world to meet two siblings in the space of a day."

"I know! I have another brother, so if you ever bump into him, you'll have the full house! Lucas said you came by his shop; I heard somebody is quite fond of cars," she said, giving Theo a nudge. "Lucas meant it when he said Theo could come by, I think he would love to have a helper for the day." This caught Theo's attention and prompted him to spend the next few minutes begging me to let him.

"I'll talk to my brother and get it arranged," Alice finally cut in, saving me any further repeated begging.

"I don't think Lucas was overly pleased with me mistaking him for Violet's dad," I said quietly, not wanting Violet to overhear in case it was a touchy subject.

"My brothers can't stand him so that doesn't surprise me. It was a bit of a bitter split. They are a little protective of me and especially Violet."

"I definitely got the protective Uncle vibes. He said he wasn't too happy to have heard Violet was hanging out with a boy." This earned a laugh from Alice.

"They're both terrible." She shook her head.

"They were like that when I had boyfriends when I was younger. God help me if they ever catch me on a date. It's going to be even harder for Violet when she's older, I'm sure."

"Does Violet still see her dad?" I asked softly.

"Sometimes. He doesn't see her as much as I wish he did," she said with a sigh. "Does Theo see his?"

I hesitated for a moment. I had avoided most of the talk about Adam when we first met. There were still some parts I wasn't ready to share. However, the more I spoke to Alice, the more I began to trust her. I had a feeling there were parts of our stories that were similar and it was nice to know I wasn't doing this completely on my own.

"No and I'm not planning on it." I paused. "We only split up a couple days ago, so it's all kind of fresh." Her face softened as she watched me speak, I could see the pity washing over her.

"Oh, Lottie, I'm sorry. I didn't realise it was that recent!" She held her hand out and grabbed mine. "If you want to talk about any of it you know I'm here, right?"

"I know, thank you." I wasn't really ready to dive into all of it, especially not in front of Theo. He had only asked about his dad once since we got here, but I knew more questions would be coming. I also needed to figure out how to answer them. "Did I tell you I found a place? They emailed me back just before I got here saying I could do the paperwork and get the keys tomorrow morning. It's only a small place, so it's a start."

"That's brilliant! So you're really here to stay then?"she asks, squeezing my hand.

"It seems we are." I squeezed it back. "I just need to sort out some furniture, we didn't really come with much. I don't have to lot to spend on it until I start getting my paycheck, but I have enough for some of the basics."

"I can definitely help with that. There's a good second-hand furniture store just outside of town where I got a lot of bits for the shop. I can ask Lucas if we can borrow one of his trucks to move it to your new place."

"Oh, I don't want to put him out..."

"Oh, don't worry about that, he'd be happy to help you, I know it. I'll text him now," she said, pulling out her phone and sending off a message.

"I am really grateful for you; you know that, right?" I gave her hand another squeeze when she put the phone down on the table.

"I'm just happy to have met you. It's been really hard moving back into town after the split. It's nice to have somebody to have fun with and talk to." She smiled softly and her phone buzzed. "He says to let him know when and where and he will be happy to help," she said, holding it up to show me. It felt good to have a plan of action for tomorrow. One more night in the hotel and we would be in our new home. We spent the rest of the meal chatting while Theo recounted his day to Violet and Alice. He was slightly upset to hear Violet got a hot chocolate and cake from me at the café, but I promised to make it up to him. The next couple of hours were filled with food and laughter. I soaked in every minute of it, giving a silent toast to the future.

Twelve

Elijah

fter my embarrassing fumble at the café, I was a few
minutes late for my shift which was extremely out
of character for me. I met Officer Daines who was
back from his few days away and performing the checks as I
arrived. He jokingly looked at his watch as he saw me come
in.

"Sorry, I kind of had a bit of an issue," I said, pointing to my
still red arm.

"Oh, shit, Eli. What did you do? Are you okay?" he asked,
his joking tone no longer present as I came closer to him.

"I'm fine, just a hot coffee incident." I shook my head, trying
to play it off. I saw the concern in his eyes as he narrowed his
gaze at me.

"Do you need to see a medic?" he asked.

I should have known he wouldn't have let me leave it at that.

"No, I ran it under some cold water. It's only still red because it's fresh." It didn't hurt as much now, anyway. He stood and stared at me for a minute. "If it's still like this at the end of the shift, I'll get it looked at, I promise." He sighed deeply but seemed content at my answer. For now.

"How were your parents?" I asked in an attempt to change the subject. He had grown up in this town going to school with my father, but his own parents had moved to Florida to retire.

"They were good. My dad gets on my damn nerves, though, never listening to anything I say to him. Sometimes I think it would be easier without them," he said, shaking his head. A moment later our eyes met and I noticed the slight panic that came over his face.

"Sorry, Eli, that was completely insensitive of me. I didn't mean–" I held my hand to stop him.

There were many thoughts swimming around my head at his words, but none I wanted to voice. I could feel the anxiety filling my chest as I thought about my dad. There was a part of me that wanted to yell at Daines, tell him it wouldn't be easier without his dad. I didn't, though. We both knew it was just a bad turn of phrase. My father was his best friend. He knew it hadn't been easy for me, for any of us, since he died. Hell, he was there just after he died, he saw the aftermath of it. He was the one who pulled me back to my senses.

Over the years, especially since we were working together now, he had tried to bring up different elements of my dad. I always shot him down or changed the conversation. I didn't want to talk about it. Every time he was brought up my chest tightened and I felt like I couldn't breathe. Even now I could hear that faint screaming in my head again. I shook it off and tried to steady my breathing before responding.

"I know what you meant," I said, trying to give him a small smile, but my lips hardly moved.

I had a lot of respect for Officer Daines. He always kept his eye out for our family after Dad died. I was only fifteen when it all happened. After I finished high school, he helped me get into the police academy. I was pretty adamant I wanted to join the force for years before and he helped me achieve that dream. It was unspoken between us, but I knew he requested for us to be partners. He never told me directly, but I knew. I guess he felt like he owed it to my father to watch over me. In a similar way, I felt that now with my family. Both my siblings and my mother were my responsibility, they had been for the last fifteen years as far as I was concerned. I would do anything to keep them safe. It's why I liked having Lucas live with me and Alice was back living in town; I could keep a closer eye on them. I guess Daines liked to keep his eye on me, too.

"Have you finished the checks?" I asked after I cleared my the throat.

"Nearly, I just need to do a few more things," he said, his eyes going back to the clipboard.

"Well, twice in one day. I must be a lucky man." The voice of Daniel Taylor entering the garage suddenly filled the space. I quickly put my coffee down. I knew he was going to irritate me and I didn't fancy burning myself again because of it.

"Taylor, Lawrence," Daines greeted them, his head turning to me. He disliked the two of them as much as I did, although he was far politer than me.

"How's the arm?" Officer Lawrence asked as they got closer. It almost felt as if there was some care to his question.

"Fine, thanks. Nothing special." I kept my response short hoping Officer Daines would be done soon and we could be on our way.

"I mean, I'd burn myself if it meant Lottie would touch me, too," Officer Taylor added with a laugh. Daines stare intensified on me now, realising there was more to the story.

"Who is Lottie?" he asked.

"Beautiful new waitress that's working at Caffeine Central now," Taylor fired back. "Clearly Weatherston was quite taken with her since he threw coffee over himself at the sight of her."

"I did not throw coffee over myself because of her," I snapped back, the eyes of all three of them on me now.

"Hey, I'm not blaming you. If she keeps sweet talking me like she was today, I might just have to do something about it."

"She was just being polite. It's her job," I countered back a little too quickly.

"Jealous, are we, Weatherston?"

"Of her? Not my type." That tense feeling grew stronger. I was suddenly very glad my coffee was no longer in my hand.

"Well, if you don't mind, boys, Weatherston and I need to get on with our work. Some of us have better things to do than daydream about women who are probably way out of your league anyway, Taylor," Daines added, giving Daniel a light hearted nudge on his way past. He wasn't wrong there; Charlotte Miller was way out of his league. He didn't even deserve to be anywhere near her. Without another word I climbed into the passenger side of the cruiser as Daines got in the driver's side.

"What the hell was that about?" he asked as he started the car.

"Just Taylor being Taylor," I responded.

"You got a thing for this girl?" My head snapped towards him.

"No, of course I don't have a thing for her." My aggravation clear in my tone.

"Okay, don't bite my head off. It's okay if you do, you know?"

"Well, I don't, so drop it." He looked at me as if he was going to say something else before taking a deep sigh and pulling out of the lot. I rubbed my hand over my face, grateful he had dropped it, but still aggravated about what Taylor had said about her. Hell would freeze over before I let him pursue her.

Thirteen

Charlotte

I hardly slept Friday night, but this time it wasn't because I was anxious. I couldn't wait to wake up Saturday and sort everything out. Alice and I had agreed to meet after breakfast at her mother's, then she would help me with the paperwork before heading over to the furniture store. Lucas was going to come down with one of his bigger trucks once we had picked out everything I needed for the new place. Alice's mother, Lucy, had kindly agreed to watch Theo and Violet whilst we got everything sorted. I checked my phone before heading over to meet Alice.

Adam: I need you to answer me, Lottie.
Adam: We can start again, it'll be different this time.

It wasn't the first time he'd said something of that accord and it wouldn't be the last. With every new text I felt my anxiety heighten. I had known he wasn't going to let us go easy, but he was relentless. My finger hovered over the block button, but I couldn't bring myself to do it. Not yet.

I arrived at Lucy's house with Theo in tow. I was nervous about leaving him with a stranger. His safety was always at the top of my list. I had sacrificed so much to protect him and it felt strange to let go of control. When we arrived, Lucy wrapped me in a warm embrace immediately, as if we had known each other forever. It was comforting, she reminded me a lot of both Lucas and Alice.

"I have prepped lots of activities for the two of them to keep them out of trouble," she quipped as we walked in.

"Are you sure this is okay?" I couldn't hide the hesitation in my voice.

"Of course! He will have lots of fun, I promise." Her eyes were soft as she looked at me. "I know it's nerve-wracking leaving them. Makes you feel guilty, doesn't it?" I nodded. "I used to get it all the time. It doesn't get easier, even when you have more children. You always feel like you're missing a part of you when you go out without them."

"Does it at least get easier with age?" She laughed and shook her head.

"I still worry about my three every day," she said with a sigh. "You just want to make sure they have everything they need, that they are happy." I understood her words. Everything I ever did was for Theo. I couldn't imagine how much harder it was with three kids. Giving him everything he needed was tough enough.

She lightly grabbed my hand.

"Alice has given me your number; would you like me to send you pictures and updates of all the fun we are having?" Tears threatened to fall at her kindness, but I pulled myself together.

"Oh no, that won't be necessary. I don't think ill of you, it's just scary." She laughed again.

"I know, darling. I'm not offended, don't worry." Lucy gave my hand a squeeze before releasing it. "I will keep you updated, but if you want to speak to him at any time just call, okay? I'll keep my phone right by me." I felt a sense of calm having spoken to her. I'd been working myself up all morning over nothing. I knew where he was; he was safe. I needed to now focus on the task at hand.

The paperwork was less painful than I expected and soon I had the keys to our new apartment in my hand. The second-hand furniture store was massive, I had never seen anything quite like it before.

There were signs everywhere talking about the low prices and I was glad for that. I was going to be spending most of the rest of the money I had aside for this furniture, but I wanted to make sure it felt like home for Theo. We picked out some bedroom furniture and Alice managed to haggle them down on price for a table and sofa. It didn't take long to have enough furniture for now. I could always come back for more once I had some more money behind me. Alice shot a quick text to Lucas to tell him we were ready.

A short while later, we were sitting on my new sofa inside the shop when Alice turned her attention to the door with a clap of her hands.

"Oh, perfect. He brought my other brother with him, too." I turned to the door to greet Lucas and her other brother, but my eyes widened at the sight.

"Elijah is your other brother?" I asked, turning to her as they approached.

"You two already know each other?" she asked, her eyes darting between the two of us.

"Oh yes, sister. They do!" Lucas said with a smirk, clapping his hands together.

I could see on Lucas' face he was thoroughly enjoying the pure shock of everyone else; he obviously hadn't divulged all his knowledge on the subject to his siblings. "Our dear brother, Elijah, pulled her over on her first day in town and yelled at her."

"You did what? Why did you yell at my friend!" Her voice rose as she spoke to Elijah.

"Whoa, why are you coming for me? I think what you mean to say is, T*hank you, Elijah, for coming to help me, your sister, move a new bed into Ma's house on your day off.*"

"I'm not buying a new bed?" Alice questioned. Everyone's eyes now fell to Lucas.

"Yeah, uhm… that might have been a lie." He shrugged shyly, looking at Elijah. "I figured given your first meeting if I told you that you were here to help her move furniture, you might not come. Plus the thought of moving all that heavy stuff on my own did not sound fun." Alice snorted as Elijah's eyes narrowed on his brother.

"Don't look at me like that. I thought it was the least you could do to help her move furniture since you were unreasonable and was mean to her on her first day in town," Lucas added.

"I was not unreasonable," Elijah snapped back. I felt like I was watching a game of tennis; my eyes bounced between each of them as they spoke.

"I think what you mean to say is, Y*es, of course, Lucas, I was a dick and am happy to help the nice lady move her furniture,*" he said, gesturing to me.

"Yes, that's definitely what you meant to say," Alice said, folding her arms, both of the siblings staring Elijah down now.

"I'll help, but I'm not saying that," he answered with a scoff.

After a tense few moments of silence, Alice stood up and directed them as to what needed to go into the truck. Elijah and I didn't speak to each other, but our eyes kept meeting as we packed everything into the truck. It felt so tense between us and I couldn't exactly pinpoint why. We had a brief moment alone whilst Alice and Lucas were double checking everything was strapped down.

"How is your arm?" I asked. He was wearing a long sleeve over it.

"Fine, no harm done," he said. Suddenly now that we were close, he was avoiding my gaze.

"Thank you for helping me with all this." I put my arm on his, causing him to finally look at me. Before he could respond, his siblings came back round the front as we quickly moved away from each other.

"All ready to go?" Alice asked. I nodded and gave the address to Lucas so they could meet us there. The apartment was actually quite near their family home, just on the outside of town. It was a ground floor apartment with access to a shared garden. It wasn't much, but it was home and had space for Theo to play outside if he wanted to.

The boys had managed to beat us there and were starting to open up the truck when we arrived. I unlocked the door and walked inside, my eyes scanning the rooms as I went through. I couldn't believe this was where I lived now. I had never had a place of my own before, unless you counted my dorm room in college but even that was shared.

I'm doing it. I can provide a good, safe life for me and my son.

They made light work of moving the furniture in. Despite it now having some bits in, admittedly it did still feel slightly barren in here.

"Have you got more stuff we need to bring?" Elijah asked, coming up behind me in the kitchen. I flinched at his sudden movement behind me and he looked down, frowning at me. I could hear Lucas and Alice arguing about how to put the bed back together in the other room.

"Not really, just some clothes and some of kitchen bits I brought with us. I'll have to get some more things later on."

He nodded, looking around the room while my eyes followed his. "I know it's a little bare, but I'm sure I can decorate it up soon," I added, feeling slightly embarrassed watching him scan the place.

"Definitely, it has promise." He offered me a small smile before taking a deep breath. I wondered what kind of place he lived in. Alice had mentioned to me earlier he owned his own house that Lucas lived in with him. A few moments passed before he spoke again.

"I'm sorry for yelling at you. Lucas said you told him that I implied you were a bad mother. I didn't mean that, you know?" He paused. "I know I don't know you well, but from what I've heard you're a brilliant mother. I just was concerned and I went about it all wrong with you."

I had almost forgotten about that aspect of it until now. I remembered the rage he made me feel at his words, as if I would ever do anything to put Theo in danger. At least he was apologising to me now. I did take a while to pull over for him. I wasn't exactly innocent in all this. I could respect somebody who acknowledges their mistake.

"I'm sorry, too. I think we both just caught up in the heat of the moment." I returned his smile.

"Definitely, why don't we start again?" I raised my eyebrows at his question. "Hi, my name's Elijah. Nice to meet you." I let out a small laugh.

"I'm Lottie. Nice to meet you, too."

"I'm surprised you go by Lottie; you seem more like a Charlie to me." He shrugged.

My heart felt like it stopped at his words. *Charlie*. I hadn't been called that since my grandpa died. No matter how old I got, I was always his little Charlie.

It was a nickname that I held dear to my heart. If anyone else tried to call me it when I was younger, it annoyed me. It was a special nickname not to be used by just anyone. I hadn't even let my own parents use it. Although as I heard it now, there was something that felt right about it. It felt comforting to hear him call me that. The nickname felt safe to be spoken by his lips.

Fourteen

Elijah

If you had told me I'd be spending my Saturday afternoon helping the woman I pulled over move furniture into her apartment, I wouldn't have believed you for a second. Yet here I am, packing furniture into one of my brother's vans for her. I can't help but be annoyed by Lucas' lie, because he assumed the worst in me. I feel like he is portraying this warped image of me as some grumpy asshole. Okay, he might have that opinion of me because I behave that way *sometimes*, but if he had told me the truth, I still would have helped. I'm not a complete monster, I just like things done a certain way. I also didn't like Lucas' little game with not telling everyone the connections. He thought he was being clever or maybe he was trying to show off to Charlotte. I'm not sure which is worse; the thought of my brother one upping me or that he might be interested in Charlotte. There were definitely some words that needed to be had between us.

We finished loading everything up and I recognised the address was just past our family house on the outskirts of town. It wasn't a terrible area to live in, but it wasn't exactly the nicest. I was called out to one of the apartments next door a few weeks ago and they looked like no one had worked on them for years. I could only hope the one Charlotte was moving into was better. She deserved a decent place to live with her son.

"You shouldn't have lied to me. You know I would have helped regardless," I said to Lucas as we hopped into the van. He smirked at me before turning the engine on.

"I know you would have. It was pretty obvious from our dinner the other night you had a thing for her, but I get a kick out of winding you up," he said as he pulled away from the lot.

"I don't have a thing for her," I spat back defensively. I hardly knew her other than the fact she clearly listens to music in the car too loud and makes a pretty decent coffee.

"Oh, you don't?" he asked, mockingly. "Oh, cool. So you don't care if I ask her out, then?" My head snapped towards him instantly. I could feel a slight twinge in my chest at the thought. I clenched my fist trying to bury it down.

Lucas laughed at my response, but didn't press me any further on the matter. Instead, he filled me in on the information he had been withholding before. How Alice and Charlotte met, her son was named Theo, and he was the new best friend Violet was so excited about. Although it all felt like a strange situation, it made me happy that Alice and Violet had made new connections. We always worried about Violet making friends, but I worried about Alice, too. Her split and impending divorce have been hard on her, although she won't divulge much to Lucas and I. I was grateful she was building a support system around herself. Although she grew up here, too, she didn't seem to be as outgoing as she used to be when we were younger.

We arrived at the apartment and scouted out the logistics of bringing the furniture in, which luckily didn't seem like it would be too difficult. The apartment was in better condition than the one I'd seen nearby, but it wasn't great.

It was a small space and felt slightly cramped with the four of us in there, even without the furniture. Lucas had told me she was currently staying at a hotel so I guess for them this would feel like a palace.

I had that uneasy feeling as we were unloading again. The feeling that there was so much more to this than I knew about. This place was barren and Charlotte seemed to have hardly anything with her. I would have thought we'd make a trip to a storage facility or something for the rest of her stuff, but it never happened. I thought back to when I pulled her over, there was hardly anything in that car, either. A few bags on the trunk at most. Why would they move into a new town with so little? Everything about it just felt rushed. Once we loaded all the furniture in, we set about trying to put some of it together. Alice and Lucas were in usual fashion, arguing about who was better at something. This time it was who was better at putting a bed together. I needed a break from the bickering and found Charlotte in the kitchen. I immediately hated the fact that I frightened her. Seeing her flinch because of me was like a dagger to the heart. Something isn't adding up. I made a mental note to grill Alice about what she knows later.

I pushed the thought aside and focused on the present. This was the first real moment we had alone together since I pulled her over. It felt right to apologise. I don't regret pulling her over, but I do regret the way I spoke to her and made her feel. She clearly has Theo's best interests at heart and I didn't have a right to question that.

There was something as well about the way she held herself. The way she spoke was confident, but my instincts were telling me that confidence was fake. She was putting on some kind of show for our benefit. It made me wonder what was really going on under that smile.

"Definitely, why don't we start again?" I proposed. I have never been great at first impressions. "Hi, my name's Elijah. Nice to meet you." I held out my hand for her to shake.

"I'm Lottie. Nice to meet you, too." She laughed, taking my hand. My eyes fell on both of our hands as I shook hers gently. I could feel the same comforting warmth from her touch as I had in the café.

"I'm surprised you go by Lottie; you seem more like a Charlie to me." I'm not sure where that came from, but it had been on my mind since Lucas first called her Lottie. It was a nice name, but it just didn't feel right to call her that. Charlotte felt too formal. When I looked at her, there was something about her that just felt like Charlie was more her.

"Could you give me a hand grabbing some of the bags from my car?" she asked. The change of subject wasn't lost on me. I nodded and followed her out of the house to her car. She wasn't kidding when she said she didn't have much–there were just a couple boxes and a suitcase in there. I watched as she went to lift one of the bags out, clearly struggling with the weight of it. I moved over, reaching out my hands to grab the handle.

"I've got it," she said sternly, pulling it closer to her chest.

"No, you don't," I replied, grabbing it back out of her hands, my hands brushing against hers as I did.

"And who are you to tell me what I'm capable of carrying?" She crossed her arms against her chest as she spoke, lips pouted in annoyance. If she wasn't extremely irritating, I'd probably have thought she looked cute.

"Because I have eyes." She rolled hers at me in response. This wasn't exactly how I wanted our fresh start to go. Before she could respond, Alice came out the front door.

"I've been looking for you two, everything's all set up inside. I was thinking maybe we could all get dinner at End Zone? It has a cool arcade in it, too."

"I feel a bit old for going to an arcade on a Saturday night," I grumbled.

"Well, the arcade is more for the kids, Eli." Alice paused. "And Lucas," she said, shaking her head.

"I heard *arcade,* so I am in." Lucas popped his head out of the door.

"It'll help tire Theo out and I have zero interest in cooking tonight, so count us two in," Charlie said, grabbing a slightly lighter box from her car. My siblings' eyes both turned to me.

"Vi will be very upset if she finds out Uncle Eli didn't want to come spend time with her." Alice raised her eyebrows at me. Apparently, she wasn't above emotionally guilting me into coming.

"Fine, I'm in," I said, pushing past them to bring the box inside.

We finished unloading the rest of the car before heading back to return the van and get dressed for dinner, agreeing to meet everyone else there.

"I am proud of you," Lucas said as we drove back to our

place.

"For what?" I questioned.

"I don't think I heard you say one mean thing today, that's quite impressive for you. I feel like at one point I almost saw you smile." I only offered a grunt in response to his words. "I think you're going soft, Officer Weatherston," he teased.

Fifteen

Charlotte

There are some people who just seem to immediately get under your skin. No matter what they do, they seem to irritate you. Elijah is one of those people. Our fresh start lasted a whole five minutes before we started bickering again. He just walks around as if knows best about everything. It's infuriating. I'm not trying to sound ungrateful for his help, but I could really do without his backhanded comments.

I was hoping Officer Sunshine would deny the dinner request, but unfortunately not. Hopefully he would be able to play nice in front of the others, at least I had them to defend me against him.

I was excited to see Theo when we got to Alice's house. He looked like he had a great day, but Lucy looked exhausted. I don't think any of us were surprised when she denied the dinner invite. I think she had enough of playing with little kids for one day. We pulled into the parking lot of End Zone and both the boys were already standing by Lucas' truck. Once we parked, Violet bounded out of the car straight for Elijah. I watched as he lifted her up into his arms. I couldn't take my eyes off the two of them interacting as we made our way over. I'd never seen him in this light before.

"Look, it's the car guy!" Theo said loudly as he tugged my hand, breaking my thoughts.

"Indeed, it's me, the car guy!" Lucas said, matching his energy and earning a laugh from the adults. "Although most people call me Lucas."

"Who are you?" He asked pointing up at Elijah. It was probably a blessing in disguise he didn't recognise him from the other day. I spent a good portion of my evening that night explaining to Theo that most police officers don't yell.

"Me? I'm Elijah." He spoke with a softness I hadn't heard before as he tickled Violet before putting her down. "Theo, right?" He held his hand up for a high-five which Theo eagerly accepted.

"How did you know that?" Theo questioned.

"Car guy told me all about you," Elijah joked. This revelation seemed to thoroughly excite Theo as he immediately launched into questions for Lucas about cars. My eyes fell once again to Elijah as he held Violet's hand as they walked in. This was a completely different side to him and I couldn't help but feel a warmth in my chest as I watched him. I guess the tin man does have a heart after all.

It took a lot of convincing to make the kids sit down and to have dinner with us first before rushing straight off into the arcade, but the promise of ice-cream won them over. The kids sat on the end of the table, likely so they would be able to run off the second they took their last bite. Alice and I sat on one side with the brothers on the other. My gaze fell to Elijah opposite me who was focused on Lucas, talking about things he wanted to do with his truck. My eyes scanned his features. I had been physically this close to him before, but we were usually arguing so I hadn't really taken them in fully. It was hard to deny that he was conventionally attractive. I would imagine he has never had a hard time getting women to notice him, at least not until he opened his mouth. It was clear he took care of himself, at least physically. His beard and hair were well kept, his shirt was form fitting. I couldn't help but let my eyes wander over him. I guess in his job he needed to keep fit, but he definitely took it the extra mile. It seems like he does that in lots of ways, especially with his work. I looked between Lucas and Elijah. They were similar, although Lucas' hair was lighter, but there was something that stuck out about Elijah. He struck me as a man who would deny it to a fault, but he seemed to care about everything. The details mattered to him; I had learnt that much from our interactions.

His eyes suddenly met mine as he caught me staring at him. I felt time stop as I held his gaze. His eyes were deep and expressive, it felt like they wanted me to dive further into them. Not just to look, but to search them for what really was behind them, to find out the truth. I smiled softly as I looked at him. His breath hitched for a moment I thought, but he didn't return my gesture. His stare was hard as I watched his eyes wander as mine had with him. I felt exposed as a prickle of anxiety flowed through me. He broke his stare as Alice asked him a question, but I still felt it.

I forced my brain to return to the present and focused on Theo, who I could tell was buzzing for permission to leave the table. My eyes met Alice's as she nodded towards them.

"Go have some fun," I said, handing them the cards for the machines. Lucas jumped up, almost as quickly as the kids, before grabbing hold of Violet's hand and running off. Theo reached over, grabbing onto Elijah's hand. "Come on!" Elijah sighed, but allowed Theo to tug him over to where Lucas and Violet were.

Alice and I laughed as we watched him begrudgingly be pulled away.

"He likes to pretend he's hard as a rock, but he's just as soft as Lucas is, really," Alice said once they were out of earshot.

"I guess that's probably the police officer in him." Alice shook her head in response.

"He's been like that since our dad died. I think he felt like he had to take on the responsibility for the family." My heart sank in my chest as I thought of my own dad. He was still alive, but we hadn't spoken since I fell pregnant with Theo. In a way I was grieving him, too. At least, I was grieving the way things used to be.

"I'm sorry about your dad." I always found it hard to know what to say to people when they have experienced a loss. There really isn't anything to say to make it any better. Alice smiled.

"It was a long time ago, nearly fifteen years now. We all cope in our own ways, it's why I like reading so much. If reality gets too hard, I can just throw myself into someone else's story. I can be anyone else I want to be." She paused. "Lucas copes with humour. He's always trying to make everyone else around him happy and laugh. Like he's trying to remind himself that there is still joy to be had."

My eyes wandered to where Lucas was playing with the kids on some throwing game. I had noticed that about Lucas; it was almost as if every other sentence was some kind of joke with him. Sometimes it was those with the brightest smiles who were hurting the most.

"Elijah, he…" Alice hesitated. "He copes by throwing himself into work and trying to keep people safe." A sense of guilt washed over me as I thought back to our first interaction. He had spent the whole argument bringing up safety and I had brushed it all off as him being over dramatic. I now have a slightly better understanding—it's how he copes, how he is able to find control.

"How did he die?" I asked softly.

"Home invasion. Dad was a bit of a night owl and he startled the burglar. I guess they weren't expecting to see anyone. Shot him straight through the chest."

"That must have been awful for you."

"Lucas and I didn't see much, but Elijah and Ma saw the whole thing. Truthfully, I am quite grateful for that. I don't know how I would have coped with the images of that in my head."

I searched for words, but I couldn't find any. I understand, though. When someone passes, you want to remember them in their happier moments. I can't even begin to imagine the images Elijah and Lucy have of him.

My gaze found on Elijah once more, he was shooting hoops with Theo.

Their joy brought comfort to me.

He was so focused on the moment playing it was the first time I'd seen him laugh. There was a genuine happiness written in his expression. My heart willed him to show this side more often. The stony expression officer wasn't him; at least not all of him. I knew that now and I wished he could remember that, too. That he could remember there was still joy to be had. Just because something awful had happened, didn't mean he couldn't keep on living. That he couldn't enjoy the life he still had. You shouldn't let the world spoil who you really are.

Sixteen

Elijah

⁂

I would never admit it out loud, but tonight was the most fun I've had in a long time. I don't remember the last time I completely let go and forgot about everything. Lucas and I spent a good couple of hours playing various arcade games with the kids. Lucas, of course, refused to let them win at anything. My mind was completely free of daunting thoughts and I was in the present. I didn't feel that constant need to look around and wonder who within the room was a potential threat.

For once I was lying in bed awake, not because of the nightmares, but reliving joyful moments. My eyes wandered to my alarm clock. It was just after midnight and would still be a while until I fell asleep.

My thoughts couldn't help but wander back to Charlie. She just always seemed to have a glow about her, especially when she is with Theo. Although they're not overly similar in looks, their personalities go hand in hand. Theo has to be one of the friendliest, kindest kids I have ever met. He definitely gets that from his mother. Violet also seems to come out of her shell more with him and I'm grateful for that. I think sometimes we need people like them to help pull us out of our comfort zone, remind us that there is joy still to be had.

I can't explain it, but being around Charlie, Theo, and my family makes me want to be a better person. I know I can be slightly uptight, but I want to be who I was tonight more; I just don't know how to do it.

I think Lucas is right. I might be starting to go soft.

* * *

I spent most of my day off Sunday at home. By the time my Monday shift came round, I actually felt refreshed for once. My mind kept going back to Charlie and that apartment. I was still surprised at how little she actually had brought with her. I couldn't help but feel a little sad at how barren the space was. I understood it was better than a hotel room, but it didn't feel like much of a home to me. I couldn't shake the feeling that I wanted to do something about it. Why did I care so much?

I planned to stop into Caffeine Central on my way into work. This was fairly routine for me anyway, but I hoped Charlie would be there. That part was definitely new. I allowed a small smile to creep onto my face as I saw her behind the counter–that was until I realised who she was talking to. Daniel Taylor had his arms leaning on the counter, leering at her. She was laughing softly as she pushed her hair behind her ear, fully engaged in their conversation. I struggled to swallow down the tension rising up in me. My fists were clenched and my heart felt like it was going to pound right out of me.

Daniel Taylor is a nasty piece of work. How he ever got onto the force is beyond me. He was always that cocky guy in high school. Even though he was a couple grades below me, you always heard stories about him. Over the years I've heard lots of rumours about the way he treats women and there was no way in hell I was going to let him do the same to Charlie.

Alice and him were in the same grade. She told me all about how he leered after the girls in their class. He would encourage them to drink as much as possible, giving him the opportunity to do whatever he wanted. Luckily, he never went near Alice.

He'd be dead if he did.

As I approached, I placed my hand on his shoulder, giving it a tight squeeze that made him jump slightly.

"Morning, Daniel." I tried to hide the tension in my voice as I spoke. "Charlie, how is the new place?" I was fully aware I was interrupting something when I came over, but I wasn't going to let it continue.

"Good, we seem to be settling in nicely." She paused. "Thank you for all your help on Saturday, Theo hasn't stopped talking about you." I felt Daniel's eyes turn to me; I hoped it was a look of jealously he was giving. I wanted him to feel how I was. "What can I get you?" she asked.

"Just a coffee, thanks." I smiled uncharacteristically sweetly at her. I may have been putting on a slight show for Daniel's benefit.

"Danny was just telling me about the summer gala." Charlie smiled back at me before turning away to make a coffee. Danny? I could see Daniel smirk as she referred to him by his nickname. The familiarity they were building made me see red.

Every year the town hosts a big gala raising money for various charities. It's mostly an excuse for the adults in this town to throw a party and dance, but they do raise a lot of money for good causes.

"Elijah never goes," Daniel remarked. It was true. I had only ever gone once when Alice guilt tripped me into going with her.

"What, really? It sounds like a lot of fun!" Charlie turned her attention back to us.

"I'll be going this year," I announced. Daniel stared at me. I have no idea why I said that as I had no intention of going. There was something about her response that just made the words come out of my mouth .

"Oh, brilliant!" Charlie said, clearly unaware of the tension between Daniel and I. "As long as I can get a sitter for Theo, I'll be there. I've never been to anything like it before, I'll have to ask Alice to help me find something to wear." My mind immediately started picturing her in the kinds of dresses people wear to these events. She was the kind of girl where all eyes would be on her. I could feel the jealousy gripping my chest.

"How about dinner this week? We could celebrate your move into town." Daniel's attention turned back to her. It was a good thing she hadn't handed me my coffee yet or I'd have thrown it at him. My eyes turned to Charlie as I awaited her response.

"Uh, maybe?" she said hesitantly. I couldn't help the slight relief I felt. "You know, childcare and all that," she added, waving her hands slightly awkwardly.

"Of course, let me write my number down for you." His

smile didn't falter as she moved her pad closer to for him to write it down. "Just let me know, sweetheart," he said with a wink, picking up his coffee. I swallowed down the bile that came up in my mouth. "See you later." He nodded to me as he turned and headed out.

"Your coffee," Charlotte said to me as she placed it on the counter.

"Don't date him." The words came out before I could stop them.

"What?"

"Don't go on a date with him, he's an asshole."

She was silent for a beat as our eyes met, her smile now faded.

"Who are you to tell me who I should go on a date with?"

"I'm looking out for you. I've known Daniel a long time. You don't want to get mixed up with him." I could feel my breath beginning to shake. I needed to either calm down or get out of here.

"I can protect myself; I don't need you to look out for me." Her voice was stern now as she folded her arms. I could feel that familiar pain in my chest as my breathing started to get heavier. Something in me was about to snap.

"You say that like you have a choice as to whether I protect you or not. Spoiler alert, you don't." My tone was harsher than I intended. Then I heard it–the scream.

It started off quiet, but was getting louder with every heartbeat. I couldn't breathe in here; I chucked the envelope I brought her along with the cash for my coffee before storming out.

Seventeen

Charlotte

I 'd spent most of Sunday sorting out the apartment, trying to make it feel slightly more homely. I didn't have any money to spend on decorations yet, but I would as soon as I could. I was happy to have a shift on Monday, just to get out of the house. The tips didn't hurt, either. If it meant I had some extra cash, I didn't mind being friendly to a few patrons.

Daniel had been lingering for a while at the counter.

He was nice enough to me, but I wasn't sure how I felt about him yet. He was hard to read. I was actually quite grateful when I noticed Elijah come through the door for his morning coffee. His bubbliness took me a second to adjust to. I don't think I'd actually seen him smile before when he wasn't being sarcastic or making a dig at me. The idea of going to a summer gala was exciting to me.

I made a mental note to message Alice about whether she would be going and for the dress code info. It seemed like a popular event from the way Daniel had described it, although that could have been a ruse to get me to come with him.

As we continued to discuss our attendance, I couldn't help but sense a slight tension between the two of them. It wouldn't massively surprise me considering Elijah didn't seem to like most people. Just as I thought it couldn't get any more awkward, Daniel asked me out. I felt myself panic, but quickly composed myself. Dating wasn't exactly the top of my priority list right now. I was trying to build a new life, not get myself into another relationship. Honestly, I don't know if I could trust a man like that again after Adam.

"Uh, maybe?" The hesitation was clear in my voice and made me feel pathetic. *Was that really the best I could come up with?* I had to give it to Daniel, he was brazen. I quickly followed it up with some excuse about childcare. Theo was quite good at getting me out of things I didn't want to be at. If Daniel picked up on my hesitation and poor excuse, he didn't give it away. He seemed to accept my answer with grace which made me feel a bit guilty. I might have the wrong impression of him. Maybe it wouldn't hurt to give him a chance.

The split from Adam was just so recent.

I have spent most of my adult life being in a relationship, it wouldn't hurt me to be alone for a bit.

I could even date around a little, a small dinner with Daniel wouldn't be so bad.

I had always dreamed of settling down, getting married, and finding that love my grandparents had, but that doesn't seem to be my reality.

I already had the child, but Adam and I never married. Truthfully, I don't think we ever would have. After Theo was born and I left my job to stay home, things had begun escalating with him.

He always seemed to be angry. Everything I did was wrong in his eyes and deserved punishment .

I ignored the lingering thoughts of the past and focused my attention back on the present, handing Elijah his coffee. Daniel may have been gone now, but the tension still clung in the air.

"Don't date him." His words made my eyes snap up to meet his.

"What?" I continued to hold his gaze, trying to read how he was feeling. The perkiness he was showing earlier had quickly faded. I wondered why he had decided to put that mask on today. It was obvious he hadn't truly felt that was toward me.

"Don't go on a date with him, he's an asshole." I suddenly felt myself become interested in going on this date.

His words left me speechless for a beat. At first, I was just confused, but then I couldn't help but feel angry. It wasn't his place to interfere in what I was doing and who I was seeing. He hardly even knew me, nor did he exactly have a track record in being nice to me himself.

"Who are you to tell me who I should go on a date with?" I could feel my tone sharpen as I spoke. The anger threatened to creep out. After everything that has happened, I wasn't going to let yet another man tell me what I can and can't do with my life. Not Adam, not Elijah, not anyone.

"I'm looking out for you. I've known Daniel a long time, you don't want to get mixed up with him."

I wished I could say I was flattered he was looking out for me, I guess a part of me was. Mostly though, I was angry. I was angry that he thought he knew me well enough to put himself into my business. To be a part of my choices. I was perfectly capable of taking care of myself and I wasn't going to allow him to think of me as some weak, pathetic woman.

"I can protect myself; I don't need you to look out for me." The last person I trusted to look out for me was my grandpa. Since then, it had been just me looking out for both myself and Theo. I was happy with it that way.

"You say that like you have a choice as to whether I protect you or not. Spoiler alert, you don't."

Before I could even respond he was out the door. My eyes wandered over to the envelope on the counter, but I couldn't bring my hands to pick it up.

I took a deep breath, replaying the argument in my head. I was trying to make sense of how we got here. That man seemed to be constantly giving my whiplash. After taking a minute to calm down, I placed the cash in the register, my hands still avoiding the envelope.

I waited a minute thinking he may return for it; I don't know if he dropped it by accident or if it was meant for me. Tentatively I flipped it over and saw *"Charlie and Theo"* written on the front.

He'd left it on purpose, although I imagine throwing it down aggressively wasn't how he intended to give it to me.

No new customers had walked in since Elijah left, so I decided it wouldn't hurt to open it now. My fingers traced the edge, slowly opening the envelope. Inside was a new home themed card. As I pulled it out, a gift card fell out of it.

I opened up the card to read inside.

To Charlie and Theo,
   Welcome to the neighbourhood.
   Figured you could use this to help brighten up the new place.

From,
Officer Sunshine

I couldn't help but smile at the words on the card and him signing it off with my nickname for him. It reminded me of how he was playing with Theo and Violet the other night. There was definitely a softer side to him, albeit his grumpy side tended to come out more often I wondered what it would take to break through to him, to truly see who Elijah really was underneath that.

As I picked up the gift card, I recognised the name from a homeware place Alice was telling me about. I had made a mental note to go once I had gotten my first pay check, but I guess now I'd have a reason to pop in there sooner. The card didn't specify an amount, but I'm sure could get something small to make it feel a little bit more like home.

I couldn't get the card off my mind. Well, truthfully, it was *Elijah* I couldn't get off of my mind. I spent the rest of my shift thinking about it. He had definitely made up from our first meeting. I almost felt bad having a go at him about Daniel. Maybe he did have my best interests at heart.

After I finished, I grabbed my phone to text Alice for his number. I wanted to at least shoot him a thank you text for the card. Instead the message I read made my breath catch.

Adam: Lottie this is ridiculous now. You think you can run away with my son? Come home or I'm coming to you.

I felt like the wind had been knocked out of me as I read it. I was certain everyone around me could hear my heart beating. I told myself to calm down–he had no idea where we were, he was just trying to scare me. I felt like everything was happening all at once. Sighing, I did something I hoped I wouldn't regret. I sent Daniel Taylor a message to arrange to meet for dinner.

Eighteen

Elijah

I felt sick.

I paced up and down the street for a minute, trying pointlessly to calm down. Giving in, I called into work, giving the receptionist some half-arsed excuse as to why I wasn't going to make my shift. I *never* called in sick. I *never* took days off. But I couldn't go into work like this. I found my way to my car, desperate to get away from all of the people around. They were watching me, judging me–I could feel it. I was in no state to drive home, but that didn't stop me. All reason had gone out of the window. Luckily, it was a short drive. My hands shook on the steering wheel as I struggled to contain my breathing.

After making my way through the door I grabbed a glass of water, sipping slowly in an attempt to regain some control. As I slammed it down, my breathing only quickened. Leaning my hands on the side for support, I closed my eyes. I tried to think of something, *anything* other than the thoughts of death consuming my head.

I thought of Charlotte. I thought of the way her auburn hair fell softly down her shoulders. Her wide smile as I entered the café. The kindness that shined through her eyes as she spoke. I always found myself trying to meet her gaze. There could be hundreds of people in a room and I would always look for her. Look for her eyes, those eyes that made me feel safe.

I then thought about the sadness in them when we argued earlier, how upset she looked with me. I had gone in there to give her a gift and I ruined it, like I ruined everything. No matter how hard I tried, I always seemed to get things wrong. Sometimes it was hard to shake the feeling that people may be better off without me.

Any fraction of calm that came from thinking of her quickly evaporated. I moved a hand to my chest, clutching it hoping it would stop the pain. My eyes wandered to the sink as I was trying to decide if I was just feeling nauseous or if I was actually going to be sick.

The screaming started again and I immediately put my hands to my ears, trying to block out the sound, but it didn't stop.

"Elijah!"

The screaming formed into words, saying my name over and over again. Trying to get my attention, but I wouldn't listen. Even though I wasn't moving I felt the voice getting further away.

"Elijah, stop!"

There was desperation in her voice now. She was trying to reach me, but I clearly wasn't listening. Her screaming got further and further away from me until I could no longer hear her. I sank down to the floor, hugging my knees. I took deep breaths, trying to focus on a singular spot in front of me, but I felt frozen. My body was stuck in place.

It was a car door that eventually broke me from the trance. I don't know how long I'd been on the floor, but if that was Lucas, it must have been hours. I quickly stood back up as he entered, trying to act normal.

"Oh, hey. I wasn't expecting to see you yet. I thought you were working late tonight?" he questioned as he threw his bag on the side.

"I wasn't feeling good earlier, so I called in sick." He watched me for a moment. He knew as well as anyone that me calling in sick was unheard of.

"Nothing contagious, I hope."

Charming.

"No, I feel better now. I think I was just overdoing it. My body just needed some time to rest." He raised an eyebrow in my direction, heading over and putting his hand to my forehead.

"You don't look so good. You sure it's just that?"

"Yeah, I'm actually feeling much better now," I lied. My breathing was back to normal, but I could still feel the anxiousness clouding my chest.

"Well, it might not be a bad idea for you to take tomorrow off, too. The town will survive without you for another day."

I nodded, but I think we both knew that there was no way I'd be taking another day off. Today was just a blip. I lost control for a bit, but I'm fine now. Everything will go back to normal tomorrow.

Nineteen

Charlotte

The number of texts I was receiving from Adam seemed to continue increasing as time went on. I could tell the different stages of drunk he was by his texts. Whenever it was early on in the drinking or he was still sober, they were sweeter.

Adam: I miss you both so much. I love you, Lottie.
  Adam: I hope Theo is being good for you?

It's when I receive those texts that I start to miss him. I start to worry if I made the right decision in leaving. He can be a doting partner and father when he wants to be...Maybe we could find a way to make this work. Once he is a few beers in, the texts started to become more desperate.

Adam: I don't know if I can do this without you.

Adam: Please Lottie, I need my family back.

That's when I really start to feel the guilt and question myself. I can't shake the feeling that maybe I was being selfish in leaving. I know I told myself it was for a better start for Theo and I, but what about Adam? Is there something I could have done to help him out of the hole? I tried, didn't I? I guess I could have done more. Maybe it isn't too late to do more for him. As time goes on and more alcohol gets into his system, the texts become violent.

Adam: Pick up your phone.
 Adam: I am going to make you regret ever thinking you could leave me.
 Adam: When I find you, you're dead.

I am reminded exactly why I left. Adam is unpredictable. Adam is *dangerous*. Whilst I know he is drunk and these are angry words, if he wanted to, he is perfectly capable of carrying it out. I have lost count of how many times I have been on the wrong end of his anger. I had been lucky that up until now, Theo hadn't been on the receiving end. But I knew it was only a matter of time before he turned on him, too. I had been careful when researching this place. He wouldn't find us here, but I couldn't help to feel a slight pang of anxiety at the possibility.

What if Adam finds us?

Wednesday rolled around and I had a couple days off from the café. I wasn't quite ready to leave Theo to work full time, so I was building up slowly until he was old enough to go to school. I just had to make sure I worked enough hours to keep up with the rent.

I made plans with Alice for a coffee and park date in the morning before she had to go to work. I debated whether or not to mention the texts from Adam. I was starting to doubt how careful I had been with our location. Adam isn't stupid. I was worried that if he was determined enough, he would find us here.

Every time there was a gap in conversation the words were at the tip of my tongue, but I couldn't bring myself to tell her. We even talked about some memories of Theo that involved Adam before, but I still couldn't bring myself to say anything. I didn't want to cause a fuss unnecessarily and I knew she would want me to talk to Elijah about it, given his occupation. I'm not sure Officer Sunshine would be overly sympathetic. I'm definitely not his favourite person at the moment, either. I told her about my conversation and impending date with Daniel Taylor. She gave me a strange look.

"You could do a lot better than Daniel Taylor." She shrugged, "He was an asshole back in high school." It was interesting to hear her say that. Maybe Elijah's words have some weight to it. Then again, most people changed a lot after school.

"It's just one date, it probably won't grow into anything more. I'm just interested in putting myself out there again." She smiled at me, but I could tell she was still unsure.

"Will you keep me updated on Friday with the date?"

"Of course." It felt like an odd request, but maybe it was a typical friend thing to do. I hadn't exactly been on lots of dates before.

"Ma is going to be watching Violet whilst I am at the gala. She said she'd be happy to watch Theo for the night, if you wanted?" she asked, changing the subject.

I had almost forgotten about the gala. I still wanted to go, but for some reason it felt wrong to be enjoying myself. How could I have fun when I had Adam looming over me?

"Oh, I wouldn't want to put her out," I answered quickly. "Does she not want to go?" I asked. Alice shook her head.

"She used to go all the time with my dad, but she can't face it now without him." My heart sank at her words. Grief always lingered, it never seemed to completely fade. In some ways it was nice because you carried that person with you wherever you went, but it was hard because you are never able to make new memories without this bittersweetness.

You were left clinging onto everything you knew about them, hoping as you got older you didn't forget anything. That you wouldn't forget the way they smiled or laughed. That you wouldn't forget how they looked when they were excited about something. You even wished not to forget the bad stuff, the way they looked when they were sad or angry. All of those emotions were who they were. They were part of your experience with them.

My parents weren't dead, but it felt like they were. They might as well be. Sometimes when it was quiet, I would lay in my bed and think about the memories. The good ones where we went to the zoo or they read me my favourite books before bed. Alongside the bad ones where there was yelling, hands and items being thrown around the room. In a way I grieved them, too, but I grieved the things they never did. I grieved the fact they never met Theo, that they weren't there when he first learned to walk. Every time Theo asks a question about my family, it's like a knife to my chest. How do I tell him they actively chose not to be a part of his life, that they didn't want him? That they didn't want me either.

How do I explain to him the reason we stayed in the situation with his father so long is because we had nowhere to go? No one who loved us enough to save us, to help us escape. I know he's only small and I'm hopeful he won't remember any of it. If he does, then I hope he understands why I stayed so long. His safety has always been and will always be my top priority. He is the only reason I found the strength to fight my way out without help. He will never have to grieve me whilst I am still alive.

"If she is sure that would be great. It would be nice to do something adult orientated for a change." I smiled, hoping it was coming across as genuine.

"Let me text her now to check." Alice smiled back before grabbing her phone out of her pocket and sending a text. "I don't remember the last time I did something adult-only that wasn't work." She chuckled. After a moment her phone buzzed.

"She said she's more than happy to. Violet and Theo can have a sleepover so we can enjoy our night," Alice beamed. The thought of not having Theo with me overnight gave me a small surge of anxiety, but I trusted Lucy. There was something about her that made me feel safe in her presence. "She also asked if you wanted to join us for family dinner tomorrow night? I think both the boys will be there, too." My smile was genuine this time at the word *family.* I had been in this town just over a week and already felt more welcome here than I had anywhere else. I had been chasing this feeling for so long and I hadn't even known it.

"We'd love to come, thank her for me."

After saying goodbye to Alice, I decided to make a trip to the store Elijah had given us the gift card for. I didn't know how much was on it, but figured we could buy a little frame or art to spruce the place up a bit. I searched around for a while and found a musical print for $30. It was an artist impression of a piano with musical notes coming out of it. It reminded me of my grandpa and the happier memories I had of him and my life. After spotting it I couldn't help but take it to the checkout to buy. Theo had also found a car ornament that he was refusing to let go of. I still had some money left over, so I decided it wasn't worth fighting him. I could pay the $10 for it.

"I've taken the total off the gift card so you still have $305 left on there." The cashier smiled at me as she handed it back. I thought my jaw was about to drop onto the floor.

"There is $305 left on there?" My voice shook slightly. There was no way that was true.

"Well, there was $350 to start with and you spent $45 today." She smiled back at me, a slight hint of confusion on her face. I didn't exactly need the maths lesson; I was more taken aback by how much was on there. There was no way Elijah did that on purpose–they must have inputted the wrong amount and he didn't catch it.

I thanked the cashier and put the gift card back in my purse. I would be seeing him at dinner tomorrow so I would give it back to him then. He could go back to the store and try to get a refund or maybe just buy himself something. This would just be a silly mistake we laugh about someday.

Twenty

Elijah

⁓⦿⦿⁓

S leep was always something I had struggled with. Being kept awake by past events was pretty common for me. It was rare, however, that I didn't sleep at all; not even for a couple of hours.

I spent all night laying on my bed thinking.

The night started thinking about work, soon followed by the thoughts about my father. Usually, I did whatever I could to get rid of thoughts of him as quickly as possible, but tonight I let them linger. I let the pain cling onto my chest, overwhelming my mind. I allowed the tears I buried deep inside to flow freely now. My sobs were so hard on my chest it was agonising. My brain worked through the timeline of events starting with the good ones, but those hurt just as much. Images of my father taking us fishing or when he would blast music in the living room as he forced us all to have dance parties with him.

He was a man who brought joy to every room he entered.

They always say at funerals about how people light up a room–he really did. No matter the day we had at school or my mother had at work, he was always there to make you feel better. You felt happy because he made you feel happy. My life has been filled with darkness since he passed, no one has been able to make me feel better.

There are moments that I feel happy, usually moments when I am around my family. I try to cling onto those moments for as long as I can, but they quickly fade and I am left in the darkness once more. The issue with my family is I've never been able to really talk to them about how I feel. Even at my father's funeral I felt like I had to hold it together for my mother, Lucas, and Alice. They didn't have Dad to take care of them anymore, so I needed to be the one to step into that role.

I didn't do the role like my father did; I don't know how he ever did it. I don't light up a room when I walk into it. There were no more fishing trips or dance parties. I did my best to make them feel better, but often failed them. The only thing I could do was make sure they were safe, that they were protected. Nobody was going to hurt them whilst I was around. I wasn't going to let what happened to Dad happen to anyone else. Sometimes I wish I didn't have to step into his place. I felt like I was going to drown under the pressure. I wish someone else had picked up the burden of holding everything together, that someone was taking care of me as I did them. Maybe I wouldn't feel so dark and scared all the time if I wasn't spending all my energy being the glue.

As I thought back to the happy days with Dad my chest tightened. When was the last time I spent more than a fleeting moment feeling joy? My thoughts turned to Charlie.

Her personality is similar to my father's. She walked into a room and it felt like there was joy again. All eyes were on her, or at least mine always were. Even when we were arguing, I just felt better being in her presence. It was a feeling I hadn't felt since he died. I didn't know how else to describe it other than feeling safe in her presence.

My thoughts had left my father now and were solely focused on Charlie. I felt my breathing slowing down and the tears soon stopped falling. I wasn't even physically in her presence and she still made me feel better. I was torn between feeling happy and feeling anxious. I had sworn off the idea of letting anyone close to me like that a long time ago. I was not the guy who asked a woman out or had relationships. I'd never once had a steady relationship with someone and promised myself I never would. Charlie was making me want to rewrite every single one of my rules and it was driving me insane. No matter how much I wanted to break my rules, I wasn't going to; not for her and not for anyone. I had put these boundaries in my life for a reason.

There were too many people who needed me for me to allow myself to slip.

Whilst I couldn't allow anything to come into fruition, I could allow myself to dream. I spent the rest of my night thinking thoughts about Charlie, about Theo, about the life I would live if I didn't have the responsibilities I had. Sleep never came, but these thoughts brought a small glimmer of light to the darkness that had surrounded my night.

The morning eventually came and I stared at the flicker of sun peeking through my curtains. I usually went for a run before my shift, but my body was crying out for rest, so I decided to break my routine. Instead, I found my way to the shower, turning the temperature up to my usual, scalding preference. This time it was not to make me feel something, it was to distract me from the many feelings that went through my head last night. I wanted the aching in my chest to go away.

Heading downstairs I noticed Lucas' truck was already gone for the day. I made a mental note to check in with him about his hours. Whilst I knew the happy life, full of marriage and kids wasn't my destiny, I wanted it for my siblings. If Lucas spent all his time working, he would never be able experience all the other things that would make him happy. I wanted him to be happy. I wanted Alice and Violet to be happy, too. I would do whatever it took to make sure they lived the best lives possible.

Knowing I was alone I found myself heading towards the piano, my fingers hovering over the keys as I thought about what to play. Usually, the songs I played were melancholic, but today that just didn't feel right. I tried to push my mind out of it and let my fingers do the work. For some reason *Your Song* by Elton John was the first to come out. Feeling a sense of calm washing over me, I played for another thirty minutes before reluctantly making my way to work. There was something about music that made life a little easier, it made me feel like everything was going to be okay. I could get completely lost in it and block out everything else. There was a power in it, I would be completely lost without it.

I spent most of my shift in a complete haze. If Daines noticed something was off, he didn't say anything. My mind and my heart just weren't in it today and I was grateful when it ended. I was grateful that tonight was family dinner, that I would get to spend time with them and forget about everything else. Charlie had been consuming my thoughts all day and I was grateful to have some family time planned to distract me from all of it. I wasn't going to have enough time to go home first, so I texted Lucas that I'd meet him there and swung into the gas station on my way. I grabbed some flowers for Ma and a smaller bunch for Violet. If I dared show up without one for Violet, there would be hell to pay.

I was greeted by Ma's famous, warm embrace as I walked through the door, handing her the flowers.

I kept Violet's hidden behind my back as she ran to the door.

"Did you not bring any for me?" Violet asked, frowning and folding her arms in front of her chest.

"You think I would ever forget about you?" I smirked, bringing the flowers round my front and passing them to her.

"You're the best uncle ever!" she squealed as she took them from me. Lucas loudly cleared his throat behind her and raised an eyebrow. "You didn't bring me any flowers." She shrugged at him, laughing as I picked her up. Lucas mouthed *suck up* behind her back.

My attention was taken away by the sound of women laughing in the dining room as we walked forward. The voice was familiar, but I couldn't place it. My eyes opened wide as I noticed Charlie across the room. Her eyes turned to meet mine as I walked in before moving down to the flowers in Violet's hand.

"Look at my pretty flowers!" Violet said loudly, breaking the brief silence in the room.

"Those are so beautiful, Vi," Charlie said cheerfully. "Roses are my absolute favourites." Her gaze lifted back up to meet my eyes again as she smiled directly at me. In that moment I felt like it was only the two of us in the room. There could be an infinite number of things happening in that room, but I didn't care. I was so focused on her.

"Careful, you're going to make her standards for a future partner ridiculously high," Alice teased as I put Violet down.

"As they should be!" Charlie interjected. "Maybe you could teach Theo a thing or two for when he's older." Charlie winked at me as she said this and I felt like my legs were about to give out.

Twenty-One

Charlotte

⚜

I honestly can't remember the last time I sat down for a family-type dinner. Theo and I tended to eat at separate times for ease; quite often my dinner was after his bedtime. Adam and I never really sat and ate together, either. Often he'd eat in front of the TV or eat so quickly so he could go out to the bar. I lost count of how many times he came home late, drunk, and threw dinner across the room out of spite.

It would be fair to say Theo and I don't have much experiences of normal family dinners.

I knew I was likely completely overthinking it, but I couldn't help it. I had spent the last ten minutes staring at myself in the mirror wearing a floral dress, wondering if it was good enough.

With time ticking away, I sighed and settled on the dress. It was just a family dinner, not a special occasion. I dressed

123

Theo in the smartest shirt and trousers I could find for him, knowing full well he'd be wearing most of his dinner by the end of the night.

The Weatherston family home was only about a fifteen-minute walk from our new place, so we decided to forgo the car for the evening.

Secretly, I was hoping the walk would tire Theo out a bit before dinner. I lifted Theo up to ring the bell and was greeted by Lucy almost immediately. She threw her arms around me and embraced me tightly. Her smile was radiating; she had such a light energy about her. It made me think about my conversation with Alice the other day about their dad. This woman in front of me suffered a huge loss and you wouldn't even know it by the way she acted. People had such an incredible ability to mask the darkness they felt on the inside, it almost made me feel uneasy. I guess I did it, too. I had spoken briefly with Alice about Adam, but never delved into the details. You can get pretty good at masking the pain when you have to do it often.

I passed over the bottle of wine I picked up yesterday as we entered the house. I had been here before when I dropped Theo off to move, but I didn't really take the time to look around before. Mostly because I didn't know the family connection yet, then. My eyes scanned the childhood pictures for glimpses into their past. One that caught my eye was a picture of all three siblings together where Elijah was in the middle with his arms around Lucas and Alice. There was pure joy on all of their faces, the epitome of innocence. Next to it was another picture of Elijah and his dad. His dad looked exactly like Elijah does now. I couldn't help but wonder if he noticed, if that fact hurt him. If when he looked in the mirror, it stung knowing he looked like the man he grieved.

"They are like twins, aren't they?" Lucy asked, noticing me looking at the pictures. "The other two look more like me, but Elijah is all his father. You wouldn't even know I was involved." She laughed softly as she led me through to the dining room. Theo and Violet were overjoyed to see each other as they bolted round the table to each other.

"Careful," I warned as Theo nearly sent Alice flying. She shook her head, looking at me and chuckled.

"You wouldn't think they literally saw each other yesterday." She sighed.

"I think it's nice Violet has a best friend," Lucy interjected.

"It's definitely helped Theo adjust to this move easily," I said. I had expected much more resistance from Theo. I tried to keep him away from the bad side of his father, so I figured he would be more resentful about leaving. Maybe he saw more than I realised or his relationship with his father was weaker than I thought. He seemed a lot happier here than I've ever seen him. I was happier here, too; That was for sure. The crazy texts aside, I felt like we could make a life here.

We engaged in conversation for a while, mostly centred around my date tomorrow with Daniel. The door rang again and Lucas appeared into the room.

"Lottie," he said cheerfully.

"I didn't know we'd have the pleasure of your company tonight." I rolled my eyes at him as he pulled me in for a hug before moving onto his sister.

"Where's Elijah?" Alice asked, looking behind him. I felt my breath catch waiting for Elijah to emerge from the corridor.

"He was working late, so he's coming separately."

Lucas shrugged as he made his way over to Violet and Theo

playing. Alice, Lucy, and I engaged in general conversation whilst we were waiting, but I couldn't help but keep looking at the hallway. I was nervous about seeing Elijah. After the tense ending to our last conversation, I am not sure exactly where we stand. I finally felt like we were getting to a civil place, with the potential for even friendship, if he could go more than one day without insulting me.

A few moments later, the doorbell rang and I tried to focus on Alice's story as I heard the greetings out in the hallway. My eyes were drawn to the small bunch of flowers in Violet's hands.

"Look at my pretty flowers!" I felt my chest squeeze at her words. A smile formed on my lips as I looked between Violet and Elijah. Every so often I felt like I was getting glimpses into who Elijah truly was. His softer side came out when he was with his niece or family in general. I ached to see more of him like this. I couldn't help but wish to be on the receiving end of it more. I know the gift card he gave us was another glimpse, although I still needed to discuss the amount error with him.

"Those are so beautiful, Vi. Roses are my absolute favourites." My eyes focused now solely on Elijah. I could see a smile fighting its way out of the corner of his lips as he met my gaze. It almost felt like a game, trying to get a smile out of him.

"Careful, you're going to make her standards for a future partner ridiculously high," Alice interjected.

"As they should be! Maybe you could teach Theo a thing or two for when he's older," I said, giving a small wink to Elijah. He held onto my gaze. The smile had won and it spread across his face. Part of me wanted to stay in this moment. There wasn't an ounce of negative tension in the room. I meant what I said—I hoped Violet always held her standards high. I wished I had a better example when I was younger. Maybe then I wouldn't have fallen in with a guy like Adam. Maybe I would have found someone who bought flowers for me or spent time playing in the arcade with Theo. Someone like Elijah.

"Well, now everyone is here, I better start dishing up," Lucy said as she walked into the room, carrying her own bunch of flowers, which made me smile once more.

"Let me help!" I said, ignoring her protests that followed as we walked into the kitchen.

"You're a guest, you don't need to be helping me," she said for what must have been the third time since I entered the kitchen.

"I like to help and truthfully, I've done very little cooking since I got here." She stopped what she was doing and turned to look at me.

"It is hard when you're on your own at first," she said softly. I felt guilt wash over me at her words. I was alone by choice; she was alone by circumstance.

"I can't feel too sorry for myself, it was my choice to do it alone." My eyes meet with hers. I watched as she reached her hand out to meet mine.

"I get the feeling you didn't have very many other options." I couldn't respond to her words and just shook my head softly as she squeezed my hand tighter. I could tell there were words on the tip of her tongue, but she was hesitant as she spoke.

"Are your parents still around?"

I shook my head again before speaking.

"Alive, but not interested in being grandparents or part of our lives." I felt my voice shaking as I got to the end of the sentence.

"Well, the two of you have got all of us now. We love being part of your lives." She squeezed my hand once more before turning to finish plating up. I took a minute to soak up her words before returning to help. When I was younger I felt loved, I felt like I was part of a family; but as I grew that faded. That feeling of family became fractured and the love began to wane. I wasn't sure how I was going to show Theo that love and family when everything leading up to our lives was broken. I tried for the first three years of his life to make that family with Adam, but love was still missing. I hoped now I'd be able to show him how it felt, that I could give him the life I'd always wanted for myself. I wiped a stray tear as I turned back to helping.

Conversation mostly lingered around a recent NHL game that I didn't watch or particularly care about. Sports had never really been part of my life; my dad was never particularly interested in it.

"You got to admit, Alice, that was one of the greatest games there has been in a while," Lucas said animatedly, almost like a child who was too excited to sit in their seat.

"My dad never let me watch hockey. He said it was for losers," Theo interjected and my heart dropped. This was the second time he has mentioned Adam properly since we came into town. It was true; Adam was a football and baseball fan through and through. I scanned Theo's face for any hint of emotion, but his delivery was deadpan.

"Well then, your dad is a loser," Lucas said quickly, his face dropping immediately when he realised what he said. "Sorry, I didn't mean that. Gut response." His eyes darting apologetically between Theo and I. My own eyes stayed locked on Theo, trying to read him again.

"Maybe you're right…" he said quietly, looking down at his food. The table was silent. The majority of eyes were on Theo, all of them except Elijah. I could feel the heat of his gaze on me as I turned to look at him. There was a softness in his eyes as he looked at me. I knew everyone was waiting for me to respond, but I didn't have the words.

"Well, maybe you can watch the game next time with Lucas and I?" Elijah offered after clearing his throat.

"As long as that's okay with you, Charlie?"

"Of course." I nodded, a slight break in my voice as I spoke. The offer touched my heart. "You'd like that, wouldn't you, Theo?" He shook his head aggressively at my question.

"I don't want to make Dad angry. He's not a nice Daddy when he's angry." The tension in the room increased.

"He won't be angry; you don't have to worry about that," I said, desperately trying to relieve the atmosphere.

"He will!" Theo insisted. "He was always angry with you. I don't want him to be angry at me, too." With those words Theo stood and stormed away as I quickly followed him out to the backyard.

Twenty-Two

Elijah

L ucas was never particularly good with his words, but tonight's fumble was particularly bad. I tried to help out Charlie with my offer, but it only seemed to make things worse. I watched as they both left the room, the rest of us remaining sitting in silence. The weight of Theo's words was heavy. Whilst he didn't say it, we knew the connotations of his words; the kind of relationship his dad and Charlie had was obvious. Even without knowing the full extent, I felt my blood boil thinking about it. My mind wandered to places I didn't want to go, to things I didn't want to see. After a few moments, I got up and followed them out. I felt responsible for the mess.

I knew something wasn't right with her situation. I cursed myself for not pressing her further. I had been trying to extend an olive branch to her since our first conversation, hoping that I would gradually make sense of what was going on. I shouldn't have waited, I should have been more outright with my questioning.

They didn't just come into this town on a whim, they were running. I felt an overwhelming desire to protect them, to stop any further harm coming to either of them. I didn't want her to feel that fear ever again.

She had sat in my dad's chair all night, not that she knew that. No one had sat there for fifteen years. I held my breath, watching her sit down and expecting to be filled with rage. To my surprise, I wasn't angry at all. In fact, I liked her being there, in my eye shot. There was something about being in her presence.

When I got outside, I saw her crouched down with her hands in Theo's. I watched for a moment as she spoke. Her voice was soft so I couldn't make out what she was saying, but he seemed calmer than before. She seemed to notice my presence as she flicked her gaze briefly to me. She spoke to Theo again and he turned to make his way back into the house. I ruffled his hair softly as he walked past me.

"I'm sorry if I made the situation worse," I said as Charlie approached.

"It's not your fault, it's mine. I haven't explained the whole situation to Theo properly. I guess I didn't quite realise how much he was holding inside." I could tell she was fighting back tears and I resisted the urge to reach my hand up to her face.

I had a question on the tip of my tongue, but I was scared of the answer. I was scared of finding out the truth. Even though I knew in my heart what it was.

"Was that why you moved here, because of how he treated you?" My hands shook slightly, but I clenched my fists in order to stop it. She looked at me and I watched her resolve crumble before my eyes as the tears left them. They fell fast and hard. I wrapped my arms around her back as a sob left her. Pulling her in close, she rested herself against my chest as she sobbed. It was clear that this had been building inside her. We stood silently for a moment as I laid my head on hers. She needed this moment and I needed her. I knew I was going to get addicted to having her close to me.

"You're safe now," I said softly. *You're safe now with me.* That was what I wanted to say. I wanted to tell her that I would do everything I could to keep her safe. I wouldn't let anyone hurt her again. She turned her head up to look at me, a teary smile on her face. I knew in that moment there was nothing I wouldn't do for her. She pulled away and I felt empty without her in my arms.

"I can't help but feel guilty. I made a choice for him to not have his father around anymore. He is growing to grow up without one because of me."

"I can tell you in my experience I would take no dad over a bad one any day."

"Sorry, I didn't mean to—"

"It's fine," I cut her off, not wanting her to feel guilty. "I got fifteen good years with my dad. I'd pick fifteen good ones over a lifetime of bad ones any day." She reached over and grabbed my hand. I felt my whole body relax at her touch.

"Thank you. I know it's not your job to make me feel better, but you have." I couldn't help but smile then. "I just don't want Theo to miss out on having a family."

"He won't. Besides, he's got all of us now." She laughed at this.

"Your ma said the exact same thing earlier." I believed that straight away.

My mother's heart was large, there wasn't anyone who didn't fit into it.

"Us Weatherstons like to take care of our own and that includes the two of you, now," I said, squeezing her hand in mine. We sat down on the bench outside, sitting quietly for a moment.

"You were actually sitting in my dad's chair tonight." My voice was barely above a whisper as I spoke. Her head turned to me.

"I'm so sorry, you should have said that. I wouldn't have sat there."

"That's not what I meant," I said shaking my head. "No one has sat there in fifteen years. Every time I even thought about someone sitting there, it would make me angry. That was his place and...I don't know." I took a breath, aware of her gaze on me. "I guess I couldn't accept that he was never coming back. I thought if someone sat there, it would feel wrong." I started playing with my hands, anxious to get the words out.

"But when you sat there, I didn't feel angry. I didn't feel like the world was going to collapse in on me because someone was sitting in that chair. It actually felt kind of nice. It was the first time anyone had sat in my eye shot for years and I was glad it was you." My chest felt lighter as each word left my mouth. She reached for my hand again.

"Did you know they say you die twice?" Her voice was soft. "Once when your body dies and the second time the final time someone says your name or talks about you? I haven't known you guys long, but I love the way you all talk about him." My eyes focused on her smile. "I bet he would have been proud of the people all of you are."

I nodded. "I hope so. Alice tries to talk about him in front of

Vi. I guess we are a little scared he will be forgotten. I wished he could have met her; he would have adored her." Sitting here with Charlie I didn't think about what I was saying; the words just flowed out naturally. It felt safe to tell her these things.

"I know what you mean. Theo is actually named after my grandpa. My father was around, but we weren't close. My grandpa was more like a father to me. I never really talk to Theo about him, but maybe I should."

Another silence lingered between us as I looked down at our joined hands, gently rubbing my thumb on her palm. Something so subtle felt so intimate.

"I forgot!" Her change of tone made me jump slightly. "I meant to tell you; they overcharged you on the gift card you got us." Truthfully, in the couple of days since I threw the card at her, I'd completely forgotten about it.

"What do you mean?" I questioned.

"Well, when I bought some bits, they said there was $305 left on there. I said it must have been a misprint. Hopefully they can refund you or at least you can take the rest of the card off me."

I laughed then, a loud laugh as I squeezed her hand.

"They didn't overcharge me, I put $350 on the card."

"You *what*? Elijah, that's crazy! That is way too much." I shrugged at her words.

"I wanted you to have enough so that you could make the place feel like home for you two." She tilted her head up to me as I spoke. "Besides, I was feeling like a bit of an asshole for how I behaved the day you came into town. I feel a bit worse now that I understand why you were coming to town." My breath caught on the last word.

"You didn't know…"

134

"That doesn't matter. I had a bad morning, I pulled you over, and took it out on you. I just hate making mistakes, and that morning, my mistake let two kids get away with stealing. I am pretty uptight when it comes to my work."

"You care a lot about your job, don't you?" Charlie asked. I offered a nod in response. "That's what makes you good at it, Officer Sunshine." I chuckled at the name. "This town is lucky to have you." She paused. "We should probably go back inside for dinner, I need to check on Theo." I nodded once more as we silently parted hands and walked back toward the dining room.

Twenty-Three

Charlotte

Three Months Ago

It was important for me to be my best every day, no matter how exhausted or busy I was. If I wasn't, then there was every possibility of something happening.

I was just a dead girl walking.

If Adam got home and the house wasn't spotless or Theo wasn't behaving, I would be to blame. No matter what, it was always my fault.

If the house was messy then I was lazy.

If Theo was naughty then I was a bad mother.

If I didn't hang on Adams every word and command then I was a bad partner.

I just wasn't good enough.

When you live every day in survival mode, you start to lose yourself. There were so many things that I loved to do that were now lost to the past.

Adam didn't like it when I went out, he thinks I'm lying about where I am going. About a year ago, he installed cameras outside of our house. He wanted to see when I was coming or going and what I was wearing. If I was leaving the house without prior discussion, my phone would be ringing, asking about my whereabouts. If the outfit I wore wasn't suitable in his eyes, he'd be calling me to tell me to change.

I know the question on people's mind, if they knew, would be why was I still here. Sometimes I told myself it was because Theo needed a father. Adam could be a good man when he wanted to. He never laid a hand on Theo, but sometimes I wondered if he would turn on him, too. Adam used to be lovely and kind to me once. Occasionally, he still was.

On the days after an argument or fight, he would bring me dinner and flowers, telling me how sorry he was. How it would never happen again. He would kiss me and take care of me. For an evening I would feel loved. In the beginning, I believed him when he told me it wouldn't happen again. Now I just enjoy the moments of calm and prepare myself for the chaos of the next day. When we were fighting, I longed for those brief evenings where I felt loved. Where I got a glimpse into the man I thought Adam was when we first started dating. It was so bizarre to grieve someone who was sitting right beside you. To grieve the person they used to be and who you wish they still were.

The truth of it was that I was still here because I had nowhere else to go. I hadn't worked since I found out I was pregnant with Theo. Adam gave me a small allowance to run errands and replace things around the house, but it didn't go far. My own money that I had accumulated in college had dwindled into nothing over the years. My parents had stopped talking to me. I'd tried to call them out of desperation a few times, but they never picked up. I was completely and utterly alone in the world other than Theo. Truthfully, if it wasn't for him, I would have given up a long time ago.

I held onto the hope that one day we would get a fresh start. That one day I would know what it felt like to be loved every day, not just the occasional evenings. I wanted nothing more than to feel important to somebody. I dreamt of the love I had always been missing.

There were some things I enjoyed that I held onto. When Adam was at work, I made sure music filled the house the way it used to at my grandparents' place. In between cleaning, Theo and I would dance and laugh, and for a moment, the house would be filled with joy. We would dance around the kitchen and I would soak up every drop of happiness in the room. I would soak it up in the hope that it would help me survive the evenings. It gave me something to cling to.

I jumped as I heard the door slam. Adam was home early. He worked as an insurance fraud investigator and had already warned me he'd be later today. I instinctively shut the music off and took a deep breath. The house was fairly clean, but I hadn't quite finished. I could only hope it was good enough. I dusted myself off and put on my best smile as I walked into the living room. My hand covered my mouth instantly as I stifled a scream. My eyes fell to his hands as I watched the blood dripping off of him onto the freshly cleaned carpets.

"Adam…" My voice cracked.

"It's not mine," he said sternly, as if that made it better. I'd seen him come home late before with bruises or drops of blood on his shirt, but nothing like this.

138

"What happened?" I asked softly as I edged closer towards him.

"Nothing they didn't deserve. Get me a towel." His tone was sharp and I knew not to hesitate on his instructions if I didn't want to be the next supposedly deserving victim. I ran into the kitchen, suddenly grateful that Theo was napping. I ran back out and wiped his hands with the towel.

"Are you sure you're not hurt?" His eyes met mine and for a brief moment his gaze was soft as he shook his head. We held eye contact as I finished drying his hands off. There was something tender in the moment that made forget the reality of the situation. His eyes moved to the stains on the floor and his gaze hardened once more.

"You need to clean that up now or you're going to ruin my carpet," he spat as all the tenderness floated away instantly. I didn't have a clue of how to get blood out of carpet.

"I'll have to go to the store to get something for it." He sighed loudly at my response.

"I don't care how, just go now and get it sorted."

"Well, I need to wait for Theo—" His hand made contact with my face, forcing me back onto the floor.

"I told you I don't care how!" His voice now raised as he towered over me. I knew better than to reply, it would only make it worse.

I looked at him as tears threatened to fall down my face and all I saw was anger staring back at me. How could this be the same man that used to visit me every day at work just so he could be near me? Or the same man who sat in hospital with me after I gave birth to Theo and told me I was the best thing that ever happened to him?

This man I once loved was now a monster. I knew I had to

leave. What I needed now was a plan.

Twenty-Four

Elijah

I couldn't help but feel like our time outside was cut short as we walked back into the dining room. I noticed Lucas throw me a glance, but I ignored him as I sat myself back down. The tension seemed to have lessened slightly as Alice talked to Theo and Violet about some kids' show I'd never heard of. My eyes flicked over to Charlie briefly, her own were solely focused on her son. My mind was replaying our previous conversation as I looked at her. I thought about what she said about her ex. I'd had a feeling before that there was more to her move than she was letting on. You wouldn't rock up to a completely new town overnight for no reason. She didn't go into details, but I couldn't stop my mind coming up with all sorts of images about the way in which he treated her. It made my blood boil. The thought of anyone even raising their voice to her, never mind lifting a finger to her, enraged me. I felt protective over her, over both of them. I meant what

I said. They were part of this family now.

I didn't speak much for the rest of dinner; I allowed those around me to carry the conversation as my thoughts raced. I thought about our hands touching, my thumb over her palm. Part of me wished I'd pulled her in closer, but the other part of me knew better. I'd made a promise to myself a long time ago that I wouldn't let anyone get that close to me. Relationships were never going to be on my agenda, and if I went there with her, I am not sure I could stop myself from making it more than a fling. Charlie deserved better than just being a one-night stand. She deserved someone who would stop at nothing to make her happy. I knew she deserved better than me, even though the thought of someone else having her was like a knife in my chest.

She was the first person I'd spoken to so openly about my father, about losing him. It was my fault, but I couldn't bring myself to say it. I couldn't bring myself to look at her and tell her that I was responsible for his death. I didn't want to risk doing anything that would stop her from being in my life. If I couldn't have her, I still wanted her close.

After dinner was finished, we all dispersed into different areas of the house. I went through to the kitchen to wash up.

"Hey, Elijah." I heard Charlie's voice coming from behind me. I turned around to see her standing with Theo slightly hiding behind her. "Someone has something they want to ask you." She gently nudged him in front of her.

"Did you mean what you said earlier?" he asked, shifting his weight between his feet. "That I could come watch the game with you?"

"Of course. There's one on Saturday if you want to come and watch with us. My shift ends at four, so I'll be back in time." I smiled softly. "We can maybe get some pizzas in for dinner if you both want to come?" My eyes shifted to Charlie. My chest tightened, desperate for her to say yes.

"That sounds great, we'll be there. Let me know if you want me to bring anything." Her smile was wide as she looked back. "I should probably get Theo back home, it's nearly bedtime. Get your coat, buddy." She nudged him towards the door.

We were alone again and I found myself at a loss for words as we made eye contact.

"Thank you for doing that, he absolutely loves hanging out with you guys. He still talks about playing with you in the arcade." I couldn't stop the smile that spread across my face at her words. I would be lying if I said I didn't take some pleasure in the fact he enjoyed mine and Lucas' company. I liked the kid, I cared about him. He clearly didn't have a lot of family around him and we had plenty of family to share.

"It's no problem, honestly. He's a good kid." She returned my smile before looking towards the door and back to me.

"I'm really looking forward to it," she said softly as she started to leave the room. I knew I should respond, but I couldn't find the right words. I wanted to tell her I was looking forward to seeing her again and having her over. I wanted to tell her about how much our earlier conversation meant to me. I wanted to tell her how I felt, how being with her was the first time I'd felt safe in years. That being around her made me feel calm again, like everything would be okay. It had me believing for the first time in a long time that life was more than just surviving the day-to-day, that I could be happy.

I didn't say any of that. In fact, I didn't say a word as she turned and walked out of the kitchen to say goodbye to the rest of my family.

I left shortly after, pulling into the drive just before Lucas. He came bounding into the house like a kid who had just eaten a bucket of sugar.

"Lottie said that they were coming over to watch the game on Saturday?" he asked, raising an eyebrow at me.

"Yeah, well I figured since you called his dad a loser and upset him that there was some making up to do," I shot back. He looked guilty and I hoped he felt bad for what he said.

"I'll admit that wasn't my finest moment. Sounds like Lottie's ex was a right asshole, doesn't it?" I only offered him a grunt in response. "Well, I can't say I'm going to complain that she will be hanging out here Saturday."

"What do you mean by that?" I questioned.

"Well, she's not exactly difficult on the eyes, is she?" He shrugged. "A pretty woman like that is welcome in this house anytime." He let out a low whistle when he finished speaking. Without thinking, I slammed my fist down on the counter. His eyes met mine and a smirk found its way to the corner of his mouth. He knew he was winding me up and he was loving it.

"Sorry, didn't mean to talk about your woman like that," he said, holding his hands up.

"She's not my woman," I snapped at him.

"Are you sure? The two of you seemed pretty cosy in the backyard earlier." The smirk now completely filled out. I paused for a moment, annoyed that he had been spying on us.

"We were just talking."

"That's interesting." He paused and I stared at him. "You see, you and I are talking right now and I don't see us holding hands, but the two of you were." It was aggravating me how much he was enjoying this.

"She was upset about her ex. I was comforting her, not that it is any of your business."

"Well, aren't you a hero." He mockingly held his hand to his chest. "I bet she felt so much better after talking to your grumpy self." A deep chuckle left his throat. I didn't bother to reply as I started to fix myself a drink. I could feel his eyes on me like he wanted to say something, but he just stared.

"Spit it out," I said after a beat.

"You know it's okay if you like her, right?" When I didn't respond he continued, "I know you're not big on talking about feelings and all that, but you need to let your guard down some of the time. The world's not going to suddenly implode because you let someone close to you."

"I don't like her so we don't need to have this discussion. We're barely even friends," I said gruffly.

"You sure there isn't anything more to it?"

"I'm sure."

He took a deep sigh. "That's a shame, because I kind of got the feeling she liked you more than just in a friendly way." He shrugged before heading up the stairs. I stood frozen in the kitchen, reeling off the back of his words.

I kind of got the feeling she liked you more than in just a friendly way.

Twenty-Five

Charlotte

I debated cancelling on Daniel, I felt my hands hovering over his number all day.

I tried to think of different excuses, that Theo was sick or I had a family emergency or something. It felt wrong to be going on a date with my ex still sending me threatening messages. If Adam knew I was dating, he would be furious. I was scared of the thought of him ever finding out I moved on. I couldn't bear to think about what he'd do.

Despite my concerns, I didn't cancel. I talked it out with Jane at work who convinced me to still go. I deserved to have fun and even if tonight was a failure, at least I'd get to have a nice dinner. Alice came over with Violet to watch Theo for me, but I felt guilty asking her. I'd thrown on a blue dress, purposely picking one with a high neckline. I didn't want to give Daniel the wrong impression of how tonight was going to go. I was barely on board with dating again, never mind taking it any further.

"Don't you look beautiful," Alice said as I opened the door to let her in. "When is Daniel coming?" she asked. I moved out the way to let her inside.

"I'm meeting him there, I'd rather have my own car in case I need to get back," I said, brushing my hands over my dress nervously. I still struggled with the thought of leaving Theo.

"How are you feeling?"

"Truthfully, I feel indifferent." I sighed. "I thought I'd be excited to go on a date again, but I'm just not sure about it all."

"Well, if you're not having a good time, text me and I'll call you with a fake emergency with Theo." This made me laugh, Alice was a good friend.

"Thank you, I'm going to head there now unless you need anything." She shook her head and ushered me out the door.

"Have fun, or as much fun as you can," she said softly as I closed the door behind me.

Daniel was already there when I arrived.

"God, you look hot," were the first words out of his mouth. I know I should have found that flattering, but honestly it put me on edge. I didn't like the way he looked me up and down as I took my seat. I wondered if it was too early to text Alice. "I just got us some water for the table, hope you don't mind; this place is a little pricey."

It took all my strength not to react with my face. I wanted to point out the location was all on him and I would been perfectly okay with Blake's, but it seemed pointless.

"Of course, no problem."

I smiled sweetly.

Two people walking into the restaurant caught my eye. It was Elijah and Lucy. It made me feel strange seeing him here when I am on a date with Daniel. Especially since he told me not to go ahead with this date, I felt like I had been caught. Although I knew I wasn't actually doing anything wrong. It's not like Elijah was my boyfriend or anything. Still, seeing them seated across the restaurant from me made me feel uneasy.

I saw Elijah watching me, he wasn't even bothering to hide it. Lucy was talking and he was blatantly ignoring her, staring out at us. I don't know why, but I reached out my hand and grabbed Daniel's as we made polite conversation. I had no urge to touch him, but seeing Elijah watching made me want to wind him up. I don't know why I cared what he thought. I laughed loudly at Daniel's terrible jokes, throwing my head back. God, this was pathetic. Even I knew that. As the night went on, I avoided looking over at Elijah's table, but I knew he was looking at me. I could feel his eyes glaring at me every time I laughed or moved my fingers along Daniel's arm. I pretended to listen intently as Daniel told me all about the incredible arrests he has made in his career.

It was clearly bullshit, but I pretended to hang onto every word. Why did I care so much about what Elijah thought?

Truthfully, this date was probably one of the worst ones I have ever been on. When he wasn't talking about himself and how incredible he was, he was making sexual jokes about me. I actually don't think he has asked me a single question about myself the entire time we had been here. He insisted we skipped straight to the main course and shared a dessert. He didn't even ask me what I wanted to share. By all accounts, this was an awful time, but my face and body language weren't giving that away.

As Daniel droned on, I found my mind wandering to what a date with Elijah would be like. I couldn't help but feel like it would be the complete opposite. He was inquisitive by nature, so I imagine he would steer the conversation to me at any chance he could get. He would want to know more about me. I wanted to know more about him, too. I wanted to hear about his career, not Daniel's. I shouldn't be thinking about another man on a date, but I couldn't help it. Daniel's company was miserable.

I let my eyes look over then, it was no surprise he was looking. I wondered if he'd even paid his mother a minute of attention all evening. She knew my date was here tonight. Is that why they were here? Did he come here on purpose to spy on me?

He had warned me that Daniel was an asshole, so maybe he had come out to protect me. I let that thought linger for a while as I held Elijah's gaze across the room.

"Lottie." I vaguely heard Daniel calling my name and turned around. He spoke again when I looked at him. "I said, are you ready to go?" *I have been ready to go since I sat down.* I nodded and we made our way out of the restaurant and down to my car.

"Well, tonight was brilliant. Did you maybe want to get lunch next week?" he asked excitedly as I got to my car. *Oh, god. I cannot let this go on.* As much of a jerk that he was, it wasn't fair to lead him on.

"Sorry, Danny." I used his nickname to soften the blow. "I'm just not ready to date right now. I really thought I was, but I was wrong. My attention needs to be elsewhere now, I hope you understand." It wasn't a complete lie, but even if I had been ready to date, I still wouldn't pick him again.

"Oh, sure. Yeah, that's cool," he said awkwardly, looking down at his hands.

I felt awful as we said goodbye and I climbed into my car. He watched as I drove off, giving me an awkward wave. I was grateful I had Alice to talk about this with when I got back.

Twenty-Six

Elijah

I was grateful Alice accidentally let it slip that she was babysitting for Charlie whilst she was out on a date with Daniel. I couldn't believe she was going through with it. After everything she has been through with her ex, she needed to stay far away from Taylor. He was no good for her, he didn't *deserve* her.

I convinced my mother to meet me for dinner, trying not to give away the fact I knew this date was happening at the same time and place. I felt guilty pretending this was just because I wanted to spend time with my mother. I loved spending time with her, don't get me wrong, but there was an ulterior motive here.

I immediately clocked them as we walked in, following the waitress to our table across the restaurant. The first thing I noticed was how beautiful she looked. I wished I was sitting across the table from her rather than him.

I kept my eyes on them the entire time. He seemed to be doing most of the talking, by the looks of it. To my surprise, she seemed to be taking it all in and listening intently. I've had to listen to Daniel talk before; most of what he says is about himself. How on earth could he be saying anything that interesting to her? I felt sick when I saw her touching his arm.

"Elijah James Weatherston." My mother's voice snapped my attention away briefly.

"What?"

"You only brought me here so you could spy on their date, didn't you?" she accused, her eyes darting to their table and back.

"Why would I care about their date?" I snapped back a little too harshly. She paused for a moment as she also stared over at their table.

"Because you wish that was you," she said softly.

"I don't wish it was me." I hoped my voice sounded more convincing out loud than it did in my head. "I don't trust him and Charlie has been through enough. She doesn't need someone like Taylor making everything worse for her." My mother agreed, but I could tell she wanted to say more.

As the night continued, my eyes were almost fixated on their table. She was smiling at him, laughing at his jokes. It infuriated me. I wanted to go over there and pull her away from him, make her have dinner with us instead. I wanted to keep her safe, to protect her. I wanted to make sure her and Theo got everything they wanted out of this fresh start. I didn't want another man to make her fearful like her ex did ever again. I didn't trust that she wouldn't find herself in the same place again if she pursued a relationship with Taylor.

I tried to eat the food in front of me, but honestly, I didn't have much of an appetite anymore.

I pushed my dessert around my plate as I watched them get up and walk out of the restaurant.

"I'll be right back, Ma." Before she could protest, I was up and out the door after them. I kept my distance so they wouldn't see me as I followed them to their cars. They were walking side-the-side, but not touching. I felt like that was a good sign. I couldn't get close to them when they were talking by the cars, so I wasn't able to hear what they were saying. I watched as he waved at her as she pulled away. *At least they weren't going home together.*

I moved quickly across the street and he looked confused as I approached. I reached out my arm and pushed his back against his car.

"Stay away from her," I said through gritted teeth. He looked at me in shock, as if not sure how to react.

"Why would I do that?" He was attempting to sound confident, but he was failing. I was a lot bigger and stronger than he was and he knew it.

"Because I told you to." I pushed him harder. "Stay away from Charlie or you won't like the side of me you see." I shoved him hard as he hit the ground. I didn't wait for a response as I turned and headed back to the restaurant.

"Everything okay?" My mother asked as I walked in and sat down.

"Yeah, sorry. Just realised I forgot to pay for parking. Didn't want to get a ticket."

Twenty-Seven

Charlotte

I was starting to notice a new problem I was having. I stood in the mirror, scrutinizing every inch of my outfit for tonight. I didn't even care this much with my date with Daniel last night. He had texted me about a second date this morning despite me declining his offer last night. I found myself irritated that he was pushing me when I already told him that I wasn't interested. It only made me more certain I'd made the right choice.

I was only going to watch an ice hockey game at the Weatherston boys' house, but I couldn't shake the feeling that nothing I wore was good enough. I wanted to look nice and none of the clothes I had made me feel particularly pretty. In the end, I settled on a floral, summer dress. I felt a little over dressed, but it was the best of a bad bunch. I had ordered Theo a Dallas Stars jersey to wear to watch the game at the advice of Lucas. I was slightly regretting not asking Elijah instead, as

I was worried Lucas might have been playing a trick on me.

Regardless, Theo was absolutely loving it, behaving completely polar opposite to how I was. He admired his jersey in the mirror with a wide smile on his face.

"Can we go yet?" he asked, bounding over to me. My eyes moved to my watch.

"Not for another twenty minutes." He groaned before taking himself back into the living room. I felt my phone buzz in my pocket and pulled it out. It was another set of messages from Adam. I had blocked his number, but he's started texting me off a new one.

Adam: *I really miss you. I want to see you.*
Adam: *Things will be different this time, I promise.*
Adam: *I just want to know you're okay.*

I wish I could help the fact his words tugged on my heart. When Adam was in a good mood we were in a great place. He could be a sweet guy and a brilliant dad. I had to remind myself of the times when he wasn't in a good mood, those were the times I needed to remember. He was dangerous and we were better off without him. My finger hovered over the reply button. I hadn't replied to any of his messages thus far, but maybe this would get it stop.

Charlotte: *We're okay, please stop texting me. You're only making it harder.*

His response was instant.

Adam: *I'm glad you're okay.*

155

Adam: Please, will you come home and talk to me?

Charlotte: I'm sorry, Adam, we aren't coming back.

I felt my breath hitch as I hit send. I could see the three dots appearing and disappearing.

It felt like forever before his response finally came.

Adam: I warned you before. You've left me no choice. I'm coming to you.
Adam: You can't hide from me forever.

I should have seen that coming; I provoked him. I threw my phone down on the bed as if he could somehow know where I was if I was holding it. I felt stupid. I should have just blocked this new number and moved on.

He would have given up eventually if I had stopped replying, but by replying I had only stirred him on more.

"I'm pretty sure it has been twenty minutes," Theo said from the doorway, making me jump. I looked at my watch. It had only been ten minutes which in kid world was about an hour.

"Okay, okay, let's go then." I rolled my eyes as I put my phone in my back pocket and tried to put Adam out of my mind.

As we approached Elijah's home, I couldn't help but be taken aback by how gorgeous it was. It was a two-story house with a large driveway out front as I recognised Lucas' truck parked in front. It was your typical family home, so I was slightly surprised Elijah had bought this place. From what I had heard, he was the sole owner and Lucas was just staying here till he found his footing with his business.

Elijah didn't strike me as a man who was planning on filling this house with a wife and kids, but maybe I was wrong. Theo knocked hard on the door as we approached. The door opened quickly and Elijah's face greeted us on the other side. My eyes lingered on his outfit of a black shirt and grey sweatpants. I don't know why, but there was something insanely attractively about a man in sweatpants. The thought left my head quickly as I suddenly felt incredibly overdressed for this casual evening watching a sports game.

"Hey." He smiled. I was still getting used to him smiling rather than scowling at me. "Come in." He moved out of the way to let us in. He leaned towards my ear as I walked past. Despite the fact that he was dressed casually, I caught a whiff of his cologne as he leaned in. A small smile graced my lips at the thought of him putting it on because we were coming over.

"You look beautiful," he said softly in my ear, sending a shiver down my spine. I turned my face towards him and was immediately conscious of how close our faces were.

"Thank you." I let a smile linger on my lips briefly before swiftly moving past him, not wanting him to see me blush.

"Well, if it isn't two of my favourite people," Lucas said as we walked through. He stood up off the sofa and I was pleased to see he was also in the same jersey as Theo.

"We're twins!" Theo announced loudly, pointing at his jersey as he walked over.

"You bet we are! You ready to watch the game?" He held his hand out for a high-five which Theo met eagerly.

"I've been thinking about it all day!" Theo replied, enticing a laugh from the adults in the room.

"It's all he has spoken about since dinner at your ma's house," I said, my eyes flicking between the two brothers.

"Well, get yourself comfy and I'll order us some pizzas," Lucas said, reaching for his phone. "Anything to avoid?" He aimed the question at me.

"Theo's pretty good with food, just nothing too spicy." I smiled back.

"Oh, and I hate anchovies."

Lucas gave a mock salute.

My eyes wandered around the living room and I clocked the piano sitting in the corner. It didn't look particularly dusty, suggesting it still gets played.

"Who plays the piano?" I asked.

"That would be Elijah." Lucas smirked before heading out of the room to make the call for pizzas.

"How long have you been playing?" Elijah was looking at the floor, his feet shifting from side to side.

"About fifteen years. I don't play much, just occasionally." It wasn't lost on me that fifteen years ago was when his father died. "Do you want a glass of wine?" he added quickly, wanting to change the subject.

"That would be great, thanks." I wanted to ask more about the piano and what he played, but I didn't want to push it. I got the feeling that if I pushed Elijah he would just shut down. I would have to be cautious with my line of questioning if I wanted answers. I decided to leave it for now.

"What about Theo? I have some juice or some soda in the fridge?"

"Juice is perfect. He's going to be bouncing off the walls as it is with his excitement for watching the game." He nodded before wandering off into the kitchen, coming back momentarily with our drinks.

"Pizza is ordered!" Lucas declared as he walked back into

the room. "Does anyone know when Alice is getting here?"

"She isn't coming, she has that date tonight." As soon as the words left my mouth, I regretted them. Both of the brothers' heads snapped up, staring at me.

"What date?" Lucas asked first.

"Who is he?" Elijah followed up with, close after.

"I don't really know; I shouldn't have said anything. Please don't tell Alice I told you," I pleaded. "She'll kill me if she knows." They both looked at me, as if deciding what to do next.

"I won't tell her, but I'll be bothering Ma for all the details," Lucas said as Elijah gave an agreeing nod. It was sweet, really, how protective they were over their sister. As irritating as it probably would be at times, I bet it was nice to always have someone looking out for you. We moved into the living room. Theo wanted to sit next to his new-found twin which left Elijah and I on one of the sofas together. It wasn't a particularly large sofa. Our elbows seemed to brush together frequently, especially when we were eating the pizza.

Every time we touched, I felt my cheeks go red. There was something about being close to him that made me lose control of my body's responses. I can't say I was particularly interested in the game; I feigned interest whenever one of the two brothers explained the rules to me. I hardly knew what was going on, but all I can say is ice hockey players are hot.

As the game was nearing an end, I felt my phone start ringing in my pocket. I could sense Elijah's eyes on me as I looked at it. The number was unsaved, but I knew it was Adam. I quickly rejected the call, a little bit too quickly as I felt Elijah's stare narrow on me. Within a few seconds, a text appeared and I felt like I couldn't breathe.

Adam: Found you. Rosehaven sounds lovely.

"Fuck," was the only word I could muster as all eyes in the room turned to me.

Twenty-Eight

Elijah

W as it completely insane that I was nervous about Charlie coming round? My mind kept going back to my conversation the other day with Lucas.

I kind of got the feeling she liked you more than in just a friendly way.

The issue with Lucas is he sometimes didn't know when he was taking a joke too far.

He seemed to be desperate to make everyone in the room laugh at all times.

Sometimes this desperation made knowing what was a joke and what he meant hard to decipher. I knew he was deflecting a lot of his own emotions through his humour, but if you dared try to bring that up with him, you'd see a slightly darker side of my brother. We all caried the grief of our father in different ways. Lucas seemed to think that if he made everyone else laugh, then maybe it would lessen his own pain. I had no idea if it worked for him, but I had my doubts.

When we were younger, Lucas and I used to prank our family constantly. It was like a game to see who could get the biggest laugh. At times, I missed that version of myself, where the focus of my day was having as much fun as possible. I had watched that version of me deteriorate over the years. Every time I looked in the mirror, it was like I was a completely different person than I used to be. The person I used to be had no place in this world. I needed to change in order to survive.

My thoughts went back to Charlie. Truthfully, they had hardly left her since family dinner and our conversation in the backyard. When everything else was dark she felt like a little flicker of light. The closer she was the happier I felt. The better a man I wanted to be. She would be here tonight in my house, and for the few hours that she would be here, the dark thoughts would be gone.

I thought about her date with Daniel, how angry it made me to see her giving him attention. Alice and my mother had clearly been talking as Alice sent me a text earlier, telling me a second date was off the table. Charlie had told her she wouldn't be seeing him again. I couldn't help but be relieved. I didn't care whether the reason was Charlie coming to her senses or my warning to him. As long as he stayed as far away from her as possible, I was happy.

Lucas' line of questioning was playing in my mind again. Was I sure there wasn't anything more to us? Even if I wanted to be, there can't be anything more to it than just friendship. I wouldn't allow it to become more than that. I'd feel lucky just getting to be her friend, providing I hadn't screwed everything up already. We hadn't exactly started on the greatest of terms. Although, she'd opened up to me and agreed to come round, hadn't she?

I rushed home after my shift to allow myself time to shower. I'd asked Lucas to make sure the place was tidy, but didn't trust his version of clean compared to mine.

When I walked in, admittedly it wasn't too bad, but still felt like a bachelor pad in here. I pulled out the bits I'd gotten from the shop on my break. Just a few candles, plants, and home-type décor to make the place look a bit more homey. Like people actually lived here rather than just slept here after working long days. I noticed Lucas watching me out of the corner of my eye and shot him a glare. I did not have the patience for him making fun of me right now.

Once everything was set out, I headed upstairs. Post-shower I found myself pacing in my room. I had two different outfits laid out on the bed. I couldn't decide between the casual sweatpants and shirt combo or one of my nicer shirts and jeans. On one hand, I didn't want her to think I put in absolutely no effort for her coming over, but on the other hand, I didn't want her to think I was dressing up especially for her. If Lucas was telling the truth and not just yanking my chain, I didn't want to give her the wrong idea.

After ten minutes of deliberating, I settled on the casual outfit. Lucas would probably make fun of me if I came down dressed up, anyway. Shortly after coming downstairs, I heard a knock at the door and immediately rushed to it. I paused slightly before opening it, not wanting to appear too keen.

I opened the door and my eyes fell straight to Charlie. She was breath taking. My eyes followed down her dress and I had to clear my throat before talking.

"Hey, come in." I smiled as Theo ran past me. I couldn't take my eyes off of her as she walked in the door. I couldn't help myself as I leaned in close.

"You look beautiful." I was suddenly regretting my choice of outfit. She looked like a dream and I looked like I just rolled out of bed.

I can't say that I was particularly annoyed that Theo decided to sit with Lucas, leaving Charlie having to sit with me. If I was being honest, I was purposely taking up space on the sofa so we had to sit with our elbows lightly grazing each other. I hardly watched the game, my gaze wandering over to her. I was desperate to take in all of her. I took a mental picture of how she looked. She had a slight rose tint in her cheeks whenever my fingers skimmed the side of her thighs, playing it off as I was just shifting in my seat. Her loud laugh whenever Lucas told a cheesy joke, followed by her immediate embarrassment when she realised she was laughing loud, trying to cover her mouth with her hand. The way she smiled when she looked over at Theo, the tenderness in her face as she watched him. She was perfect. The more I watched her the more I knew I was in trouble. My feelings for her were going beyond friendly.

A phone buzzing snapped me out of my thoughts and I watched as she rejected a call from an unknown number. I tried to focus on the TV so it wasn't obvious I was watching her.

"Fuck." Her voice was soft but there was a sense of fear in it. We all turned to look at her.

"You told me we can't say that word!" Theo was the first to chime in.

"Everything okay?" I asked.

"Yeah, sorry just messed something up on my phone." She replied a little too quickly. She may have a smile on her face, but the tension in her voice was obviously. Lucas and Theo turned themselves back to the game, but I kept my eyes on her. Looking at her, I pointed my head towards the kitchen door, motioning her to follow me before getting up. After she walked in, I shut the door behind us.

"Are you okay?" I asked, leaning against the door of the kitchen.

"Yeah, of course." She smiled sweetly at me and my breath hitched for a moment before I caught myself.

"Are you lying?"

She hesitated for a second. "I might be…" Her voice lowered.

"I'm a pretty good listener if you want to talk about it."

Twenty-Nine

Charlotte

I felt sick as I stood in the kitchen with Elijah. My mind was all over the place and I knew I needed to tell someone. I was scared. I was scared of what Adam would do when he found us. He would be angry, that was for sure. I left in the middle of the night with his son, of course he would be angry. This was a dangerous man with a violent past who was heading straight into town to find Theo and I. I tried to speak, but I just stuttered.

"Take your time." Elijah's voice was soft as he spoke. The tears fell then as I looked at him. In a flash he was wrapping his arms around me, pulling me close to him. I sobbed into his chest, trying not to be too loud with Theo right next door.

"Whatever it is, Charlie, we are going to fix it. I promise. We will sort it out together, okay?" His hand moved gently to my chin, lifting it up so I was looking at him.

"It's Adam," I finally managed. His face narrowed as he

looked at me. "He knows where we are." My voice was barely above a whisper. I didn't want to say it out loud. I didn't want any of this to be happening right now. I finally felt like everything was going well for us and it was crashing down right in front of my face.

"Are you sure?" I offered him my phone in response. He moved part of his body away from me to look at the messages. His eyes widened as he scrolled through the recent messages.

"How long has he been sending you messages like this?" His voice remained at a level volume, but I could sense the tension in it.

"He started a day or so after I moved into town." I leaned back so I could see Elijah's face better. He looked furious as he finished looking through the messages.

"Why didn't you tell me?" He paused. "Or Alice, or anyone?" I shook my head at him.

"I thought Adam was just trying to scare me. I didn't think he would actually figure out where we were." I sighed. "I thought I had it all handled."

His eyes moved from my phone to me briefly before he turned back to my phone and started typing.

"What are you doing?" I asked, feeling a slight panic rise in my chest.

"Adding mine and Lucas' numbers to your speed dial." He finished typing and handed me back my phone. "I want you to be able to contact us quickly should you need to. Call me first." I didn't really know what to say so I stared at him for a moment.

"I want you two to stay here tonight," he continued. I tried to object, but he cut me off. "Please, either you two stay or I am going to have to camp outside your place." I let out a teary laugh in response to that. "I can't let you guys leave here tonight knowing that he might show up at your door. Don't make me beg you to stay."

I chuckled softly at his words and nodded. "Okay, as long as you're sure. We can crash on the couch or something just for tonight." I was grateful for the offer. The thought of being alone in my apartment was terrifying. I would feel a lot safer knowing Elijah and Lucas were in the house with me. Theo would be safer, too.

"You two can take my room."

"Absolutely not. We are not kicking you out of your room."

"It's not up for discussion, Charlie. I'd rather be closer to the front door." He hesitated. "Just in case." He didn't need to explain his meaning; just in case Adam somehow figured out we were here. I guessed it was hard for him to switch that police officer nature off, I was extremely grateful for it now, though. I wanted Elijah to protect me, to keep us safe.

He moved closer to me now as he wrapped his arms around my back. I lifted mine up and placed them around his neck as he pulled me in for a hug. His hands rubbed my back softly as I held onto him tighter. An intimate silence filled the room as we just stood there for a moment.

"You're safe with me, Charlie," he whispered into my ear, making the hairs on my neck stand up.

"I'm scared of what he will do." My voice cracked as I spoke. I was trying to fight more tears that were threatening to fall. He moved away from me slightly and planted a kiss on my forehead as I melted into him.

"I won't let anything happen to either of you, I promise." We stayed in our embrace for a moment before shouting came from the other room. The game must be over now, and judging by the shouting, it was a win. We pulled away from each other and headed into the other room. I caught myself in the mirror on the way. It wasn't too obvious I had been crying.

Upon re-entering the living room, we were greeted with the sight of Lucas with Theo on his shoulders, running around shouting, "We won!" For a moment I was completely distracted from everything else that was going on and laughed at the sight. I caught Elijah out of the corner of my eye who was laughing, too. The tension I was holding in my shoulders began to ease. We were safe here, at least for now, and Theo was the happiest I had ever seen him.

"So, you enjoyed your first game then?"

I asked as I approached them.

"It was amazing!" Theo responded as Lucas lowered him onto the sofa. "Can we watch another one here next week?" he asked eagerly.

"You're more than welcome to watch all of them with us." Elijah's voice came from behind me.

My heart leapt at his comment and the sincerity in his voice.

"Both of you," he added.

"I'd really like that. Mommy, can we?" His bright eyes looked up at me.

"I'm sure we can make it work, as long as we don't start to get on the boys' nerves!" I added with a chuckle.

"Never," Lucas and Elijah said simultaneously as they exchanged a look.

A small smile passed on both of their lips. Almost as if they have an unspoken agreement.

"We enjoy having you here," Elijah added, ruffling Theo's hair before sitting back in his original seat.

"That we do," Lucas agreed. "As you can imagine, it's not

much fun for me in this house with grumpy guts over here." He placed a mocking hand to his chest before Elijah kicked him as Lucas walked past. There was a jovial atmosphere in the room as we settled back into our original seats. Conversation about the game continued and Theo was trying desperately to keep awake. Every so often his head would lull and his eyes would close before jolting awake again. Eventually he gave in and fell asleep next to Lucas.

"Charlie and Theo are staying here tonight," Elijah said bluntly. He wasn't asking a question, merely just stating this information to Lucas. I guess it was his house so he didn't feel the need to ask permission or he knew Lucas wouldn't object.

Lucas nodded.

"Makes sense, it's getting pretty late. You want to take my room? I don't mind the couch." Lucas' words made me smile. He was always offering help to others without a second thought. Although they were different in many ways, Elijah and Lucas always seemed to put others before themselves. I wondered if their dad had been like that as well.

"No, they are staying in my room," Elijah said, shaking his head. "You're working tomorrow, I'll take the sofa." Lucas didn't object. I got the feeling from Alice that Lucas worked a lot of hours and very rarely took the day off, even though tomorrow was Sunday.

We spoke for a while longer before Lucas announced he was going to bed.

"Thank you, both of you, for what you guys did for Theo tonight." I moved my gaze between the two of them. "I think he has found it hard adjusting to life without his dad and I know tonight meant the absolute world to him."

"Don't you start making me cry before bed," Lucas teased.

170

"He's a good kid, Lottie. You've done a great job with him."
Elijah nodded in agreement. I felt Elijah's hand move on top
of mine as he gave it a gentle squeeze.

"You know if there is anything we can do to make this
transition easier for him, for both of you, just ask," Elijah said
as he squeezed my hand again.

"I'm a pretty good uncle," Lucas said, holding his hands in
the air. "If you don't believe me, ask Violet." I laughed at his
comment. "If the little man or you need anything from us,
we're here," he added, gesturing to Theo. My heart felt full
in that moment. I was worried that Theo would miss out if
I moved him away, but I think he was about to gain more
than he'd bargained for with the Weatherstons. I felt like I
finally had a family again, a proper one this time. Lucas bid
goodnight before heading up the stairs and Elijah and I were
left in silence.

"I should probably get him up the bed, too," I said, rising to
my feet.

"Let me carry him up for you." He brushed past me towards
Theo, scooping him up in his arms. I couldn't help but notice
how small Theo looked in his arms. "It's the first door on the
left at the top of the stairs." I nodded and led the way up. Elijah
seemed nervous, like Theo was the most fragile thing he'd ever
held. It was sweet to see.

I felt a sense of childish excitement as I entered Elijah's
bedroom. I opened the door and let him in first with a sleeping
Theo in his arms. I watched as he gently placed him down,
pulling the covers over him. Elijah was a large guy with a hard
exterior, but in this moment, there was something soft and
tender about him. He was miles away from the man I first met.
After tucking him in, Elijah moved towards me, placing his

hand softly on my back as he moved past me.

"Do you need anything else?" he asked in a low voice, pausing at my side. I shook my head in response. "I'm just downstairs if you need me." He started to walk out the door, but hovered his hand, lightly gracing the frame.

"Goodnight, Charlie," he said softly, turning his attention to me. His nickname for me made my chest jolt every time.

"Goodnight, Officer Sunshine." I gave a mock salute and he chuckled lightly as he closed the door quietly behind him.

My attention now turned to his room, trying to take it all in despite there being hardly any light. His room was just as meticulous and organised as I expected it to be. It was clear everything had its own place. Clutter was not allowed in Elijah's bedroom. My eyes were drawn to some photos on his chest of drawers. There was one with his dad, Elijah must have been Theo's age in this photo. He was sat on his knee, grinning ear to ear. Next to that one there was a photo of Violet and Alice, followed by a photo of the two brothers lifting their mother up, bright smiles all around. It warmed my heart to see these photos. I felt this represented Elijah the best. He liked to pretend he was closed off and cold, but he loved his family more than anything. You could tell they meant the absolute world to him. Underneath everything, Elijah was kind and thoughtful. I wished the world could see him how I did, how his family did. I wished he could show everyone who he really was rather than hiding behind a mask. I felt honoured to even get a snippet into this version of Elijah.

I grabbed a long shirt out of his wardrobe and got changed. Making my way over to the bed, I got in beside Theo, snuggling down. The sheets smelt like Elijah's cologne and I buried my face into the covers as I settled in. There was something comforting about the smell. I tried to ignore the thoughts of Adam; we were safe here in this house. I could deal with everything else tomorrow.

Thirty

Elijah

⚜

As I laid down on the couch, I couldn't help my mind from racing about the situation with Charlie's ex. *Adam.*

My anxiety meant that I played out every single different scenario that could happen. They varied from me sitting down politely with him to killing him. Truthfully, I favoured the latter option. I couldn't help as well to play out all the potentially bad things that could happen to Charlie and Theo. I felt my chest tighten at the thought of losing either of them. My breathing started to become more erratic. I sat up in an attempt to gasp for air. This was not the time for a panic attack. I lowered my head into my hands and tried to focus on happier thoughts. The frequency of these attacks in the past couple of weeks was starting to grate on me. No matter how hard I tried to pull it together, I continued to fall apart. The intensity of the worry I felt overwhelmed me and I was starting to struggle with even the most basic things in my day to day.

I cast my mind back to earlier in the day to Lucas and Theo messing about. I've always thought that Lucas would make a great dad. He has this natural instinct for it and has always lit up the room. I'm not sure that I have that instinct. When Theo's around I get nervous that it's obvious I'm not a natural with kids. I find myself wanting Charlie to see potential in me when she is around and not the obvious flaws that I am nothing like my brother. I want Theo to like me, to feel like he can have fun with me and that he is safe. I find myself constantly questioning other people's feelings about me. Any actions I make, I question them for the rest of the day on whether it was the right call. Did I pay enough attention to Theo? Did I involve myself in enough of the conversation that happened? Was my joke funny?

The more I question my actions the further I find myself retracting into myself. If I keep myself quiet or cold, then people won't start judging who I really am. I don't want people to see beyond the mask, beyond what I allowed them to see.

Charlie was starting to become a problem. Every time I was with her, I felt a little part of my mask break off. I found myself wanting to let her in, to see who I really was, the parts of myself I had buried years ago. I worried if I let the mask slip, she wouldn't like who I was and I'd lose her forever. She had only been in my life a short time, but it crushed me to think of her not being in my life anymore. I wanted her close to me. *I needed her.*

Since my dad died, my life has been clouded in darkness. If it wasn't for my family, I would have given up a long time ago. I survived for them.

With Charlie around, for the first time in my life I thought, about more than just my survival. *I felt hopeful.* That maybe I could have a normal life. That maybe there was more to life than just my duty. I wanted to do more than just go about my day-to-day life, I wanted to *live*.

I kept my thoughts on Charlie, my mind replaying every moment we have had together as I slowed my breathing down. I thought about the way her hand felt in mine, how calm I felt when she was close to me. Eventually, my breathing returned to normal and I was able to lay down. I allowed the thoughts of Charlie to continue as I drifted off to sleep.

* * *

The sound of Lucas coming down the stairs woke me up the next morning. In his defence, I was still a light sleeper.

"Sorry." His voice hushed as he sat on the other couch.

"Don't worry, you off already?" He nodded.

"I have a lot of paperwork I need to get done." He sighed. I could see in his eyes he hadn't slept very well.

"You really need to hire someone else to do that."

"Cathleen does some of it for me." He shrugged.

"Someone full-time, Lucas." My voice was stern; I wasn't afraid of pulling my older brother voice out when I needed to. He ignored me and continued to lace up his boots. I don't know what it would take to get him to slow down. I know I was a big hypocrite in that department, but he had more going for him than I did. Lucas was husband and dad material. He deserved to have his happy ever after, unlike me. I didn't deserve anything close to the sort. Not after everything I had done. I felt that tightness in my chest again and attempted to shrug it off.

"Tell Charlie and Theo I said bye when they wake up," he said as he headed towards the door. I nodded in response as I stood up to go make myself a coffee.

My mind suddenly remembered that Charlie was upstairs.

Not only, that she was upstairs in *my bed*. I couldn't help but enjoy that thought. Charlie Miller was not only in my house, but in my bed right now. Okay, maybe not in the capacity I would like her to be, but she's there.

A little while after Lucas left, I heard footsteps on the stairs and turned around to see Theo making his way down cautiously.

"You okay, bud?" I asked turning in my seat.

He nodded as he made it to the last step. "Yeah, Mommy's still sleeping." I watched as he looked around the living room. "Can I have some juice?"

"Sure," I said, getting up from my seat. I make my way into the kitchen with Theo close behind. "Do you want something to eat, too? Maybe some pancakes?" I started to look around the kitchen, hoping I had the ingredients to go through with my suggestion.

"Yeah!" Theo's eyes lit up at the prospect of pancakes. "Can I help? I always help Mommy make them." I pulled up a chair next to me and helped him onto it.

"Sweet or savoury?" The correct answer was sweet, but I asked anyway.

"Sweet, obviously." He rolled his eyes.

"Obviously," I mused with a laugh. *I knew I liked this kid.* I pulled out all the ingredients and placed them on the counter in front of us. I helped Theo pour everything into the mixing bowl.

My childish instinct kicked in and I couldn't resist flicking flour at him, enticing a loud giggle from him. I had met my match, however, as he immediately grabbed a handful and threw it straight at my mouth. I half laughed and half choked in response.

What happened next can only be described as chaos as several more handfuls of flour were thrown from both sides. I grabbed hold of him, lifting him off the chair and turning him upside down as I tickled him. He attempted to shout at me to stop in between laughs.

Thirty-One

Charlotte

I awoke to the sound of laughter in the house. One giggle definitely belonged to Theo whilst the other one sounded interestingly like Elijah.

I made my way downstairs following the sound of laughter into the kitchen.

My eyes widened as I saw flour everywhere and Elijah holding Theo upside down, tickling him. They both went silent and froze at the sight of me.

"If we stay still maybe she can't see us," Elijah whispered, a devilish grin plastered on his face.

"She can see you and she can see the mess you've been making, as well." I crossed my arms trying to look annoyed, but I couldn't help but laugh. I couldn't get over how sweet this moment was. I hadn't heard Theo laughing that loudly in a while. There was something so comforting about hearing Elijah laugh, too.

"What were you boys attempting to do?" I questioned, suddenly conscious I was only wearing a long t-shirt. I unfolded my arms and pulled the material down. Luckily, Elijah was a lot taller than me and it nearly came down to my knees.

"We were—"

"Are!" Theo interrupted.

"We *are*," Elijah corrected himself, "making pancakes for breakfast." He turned Theo back the right way and placed him standing on the chair by the counter.

"I might be wrong, but I think you're supposed to put the ingredients in the bowl, not all over the kitchen?"

"Don't you question my methods, Charlotte." His use of my full name made me snort with laughter.

I raised my hands defensively. "Now, if you don't mind leaving the chefs to work their magic, we will bring it through to you." Laughing I made my way into the living room and waited for whatever they were going to create together. Over the next few minutes, all I could hear was hushed voices mixed in with the occasional giggle before the door opened. Elijah held it open as Theo walked out with a surprisingly good-looking pancake covered in chocolate and fruit. I moved myself to the table as it was presented to me.

"Well, this doesn't look anywhere near as poisonous as I was expecting," I said, cutting a piece off and taking a bite. I was genuinely shocked at how good it tasted; Elijah wasn't too bad of a cook it seemed. "My compliments to the chefs," I said teasingly after finishing my mouthful. Elijah helped Theo into a different seat before going back into the kitchen to get their portions. Theo chatted about how much he loved watching last night's game as we all tucked into our breakfasts. It was surprising how normal this all felt; the three of us chatting over breakfast. There was no awkwardness or tension, I just found myself just enjoying the company. After we'd finished my eyes wandered over to the piano.

"Did I tell you my grandpa played the piano?"

I asked. Elijah's eyes followed mine to the piano, shaking his head. "He used to play for me all the time when I was a kid." The conversation was briefly interrupted by Theo asking to be excused to watch the TV. Elijah stood up and set it up for him before returning to the table.

My eyes watched Theo; content he was too distracted by the TV to hear us talk. I continued, "My grandpa is actually the reason I finally left Adam." I softened my voice. Elijah's eyes met mine and there was some confusion in his look. I had forgotten I told him about the fact my grandpa had passed, so that probably didn't make sense.

"He left me a letter when he died," I said, anticipating his questions. "Hold on, it's in my bag." I looked around for my bag, locating it just next to the sofa. Pulling out the letter, I handed it to Elijah. It felt personal to let him read this. I hadn't ever let anyone read this letter, not even my parents. Yet here I was, handing it over to Elijah without a second thought. I watched his expression as he read the letter, but he kept it fairly neutral, not giving away his thoughts. When he finally finished reading, he looked at me again.

"I see where you get it from." He smiled softly.

"Get what from?"

"Your kind heart." I felt my cheeks turn red at his words as I looked away from him. I could feel his gaze burning into me, but I couldn't bring myself to return it. "It calms me," he continued. My head finally snapped up. "Playing the piano. It

181

calms me." I could sense a slight shake in his voice as he spoke. It was clear that this was a big thing for him to admit to me. I tried to find the best thing to respond to him, but I felt words fell short.

"I get kind of…" He hesitated. "Nervous sometimes, but when I play, I forget about everything else that is going on. Truthfully, I don't know where I would be without it." He was the one to look away now, staring down into his hands to avoid my eyes. "I've never actually told anyone that before." There was a surprise in his voice, like he couldn't quite believe he was telling someone about it.

"Thank you for trusting me enough to tell me." I choked a little bit as I spoke, struggling to get the words out whilst trying not to sound emotional. I was emotional, but I didn't want to make him regret opening up to me. "My grandpa always said it made him feel better when he played, especially for us." I was smiling wide now at the memory.

"Do you play?" He asked. I shook my head in response.

"He tried to teach me, but I guess I just didn't have the knack." I shrugged. I wished I could have picked it up, but my coordination just didn't seem to have what it needed to play. "I miss the sound of him playing. When I reread that letter all I could think about was how much I missed the sound of a piano." I wiped away a stray tear as I spoke. "I miss him."

"I could play for you?" he offered after a beat, the hesitation in his voice was clear. Our gazes met once more and I struggled to hide the emotion from my face. Given how the topic was brushed off last night, I knew this was something precious to him and here he was letting me into it.

"I'd love that." I paused. "But you don't have to if you don't want to." I didn't want him to feel like I was invading his privacy, a personal tool he used to calm himself down.

"I want to."

His voice had more certainty to it now, his confidence in sharing this information was growing. He stood up and made his way over to the piano.

I followed him cautiously trying not to stand over him.

"What songs did your grandpa used to play?"

"A mixture, really. Billy Joel was always my grandma's favourite." It was always one of mine, too.

Elijah reached into the stack of books next to the piano before pulling out a music book of Billy Joel's songs and showing it to me.

"I came prepared, it seems." He smiled as he flicked through the pages.

"Sorry, I'm not quite as impressive as your grandpa by being able to play by heart, but I've played this one a few times." His fingers found their way to the keys and it only took me a few moments to know exactly which song he was playing. *Just The Way You Are*, my grandma's favourite song. I became emotional listening to him play and I was struggling to hold my tears back. Elijah looked more relaxed than I had ever seen him as he played and it was beautiful. *It was effortless.*

I managed to get a grip on myself before he finished the song. As his fingers played the final keys, he turned to look at me. I suddenly lost myself again and let out a small sob.

"Thank you." I managed after a moment. He stood up from his seat and lightly placed his fingers on my waist. "Sorry, I didn't mean to get all emotional on you. That was my grandma's favourite song." I sniffed.

"She had good taste. It's one of my favourites, too." He pulled me in for a hug and I buried my face in his chest, more sobs following suit as memories of my grandparents flooded my brain. I don't think I realised how lonely I'd been without them. How much I missed having them look out for me.

"Mommy, are you okay?" Theo's voice came from beside me. I had almost forgotten he was in the same room. I felt Elijah move away before he picked Theo up.

"Your mommy's all good, buddy, you don't have to worry," he said, facing Theo towards me. I wiped the tears from my face and nodded in agreement.

"I'm okay. Elijah was just playing me a song and it made me think of something a bit sad, is all."

"Maybe you should play something more upbeat," Theo suggested, turning now to Elijah.

"I think that's a brilliant idea." He placed Theo back down on the floor and returned to his

seat by the piano. He closed the book and started playing. I didn't recognise the song, but it was far more upbeat. I watched him for a moment, he was smiling as he played. I felt Theo grab my hand and start dancing in the room. Laughing, I joined in with as we danced around the living room.

Truthfully, I didn't want to leave, but after a few more songs and dances with Theo, I had to start getting ready. I was working in the café this afternoon and needed to get changed and drop Theo off at day care before my shift started. There was a slight sense of awkwardness at the door when we were saying our goodbyes.

"You know you can stay here any time you want. If you're feeling unsafe or just want somewhere else to go." He folded his arms as he spoke.

"Thank you, I appreciate you letting us stay." I was conscious we hadn't spoken about Adam this morning; I didn't want to spoil the fun we were having.

"Promise me you'll call me if you're worried about anything, it doesn't matter how minor. I'll be there," he said sternly and I nodded. "Don't hesitate, Charlie."

"I promise." I moved in for a hug which he accepted without hesitation. Theo moved and grabbed onto his leg. I looked down and saw Elijah ruffle Theo's hair.

As we said our goodbyes, Theo grabbed my hand as we walked down the street towards my car.

I pulled up in our road. As much as I didn't want to work, I was looking forward to having a distraction. We both did a quick change before heading back out the door again. When we walked out, I couldn't help but feel like something was off. I felt the hairs standing up on the back of my neck as my eyes were drawn to a car going slowly past us. I recognised it immediately. *It was Adam's car.* Suddenly, the car gained speed and went round the corner, out of sight. I stood frozen for a moment as I waited to see if it would return, but it didn't. I couldn't help but feel like that was a warning.

Adam was coming for us.

Thirty-Two

Elijah

W as it completely insane that I was going to see Charlie just a couple hours after she left my house? I had absolutely no reason to go to the café today, but here I was. I'd texted Alice to ask if she wanted to meet up for a coffee so it would seem pre-planned and not something I'd organised, because I was desperate to see Charlie again.

I arrived first.

The café was fairly empty for a Sunday afternoon. Charlie and Jane were chatting at the register when I walked in.

"Well, if it isn't my favourite police officer," Jane said, smiling as I approached. "You eating today or just a coffee?"

"Just a coffee, please. Oh, actually two. Alice is meeting me here."

"Please tell me she's bringing her adorable little girl." Jane raised her eyes at me.

"Sadly, not this time, J, but I'll bring her in with me sometime soon." I looked over at Charlie and smiled, which she returned.

"I'll do these, Lottie. Do you mind clearing some of the tables?"

"Of course." She threw me another smile before walking over to the other side of the room. Jane's eyes narrowed in on me.

"Did she tell you about her ex?" Jane's voice was hushed now as she spoke.

"Yeah," I grunted out. "I read some of the texts he's been sending her."

Jane shook her head. "It's awful. Can you believe he was hanging outside her house today?"

"He was what?" I said a little too loudly. He was outside her house and she didn't call me. She promised me she would call me. I was angry now and I felt my fists clench as I steadied my breathing.

"When she was leaving for work, she said a car drove past them real fast. She was sure it was him."

"Why didn't you tell me he was outside your house?" My voice was raised now as I turned to Charlie on the other side of the room. I was lucky the place was basically empty because I was definitely making a scene.

"I don't know for sure it was him," Charlie said, harshly as she walked across the room. "There was no point worrying you."

"I am *already* worried, Charlie." I heard the door chime, but continued, "I am worried something is going to happen to you or Theo. I am going to worry until I know that he can't hurt you anymore."

"What's going on?" The sound of Alice's voice came from behind me. Charlie and I looked at each other.

"Theo's dad, Adam. He's been harassing me over text since I moved here and I think I saw him earlier by our place."

"Shit, Lottie! Why didn't you say anything?" Alice came up beside me now. I was grateful she was on my side on this one.

"I only told Elijah last night when I realised Adam knew what town we were in. I didn't think it would escalate like this." Alice embraced Charlie and I waited until they parted before speaking.

"Charlie, you promised me you would call me." She looked guilty at me. I could see the regret in her eyes.

"I'm sorry, I should have called you." I moved closer to her, not caring that Alice and Jane were watching, as I lightly graced her waist with my hand.

"Promise me again. I need you to mean it this time," I said softly, using my other hand to lift her chin so she looked up at me.

"I promise, I really mean it." Her voice matched mine. I moved away, satisfied with her response.

"I need the details of Adam's car; I'm going to put a watch on it." She nodded and grabbed her notepad out of pocket, writing down the details. I'd camp outside her place 24/7 if I had to. I wasn't going to let him hurt her. I wasn't going to let him take her from me. She was mine to protect now. After she wrote it down, she moved away to finish clearing up the tables. Alice raised her eyebrows at me when I turned to face her. I knew what that look meant; she knew she was missing some of the pieces. We grabbed our coffees and headed to a table at the back.

"You two look…" She paused. "Cosy." I wasn't really in the mood to have this conversation. All I could feel was panic about the situation. I didn't know what to do. At the moment there was nothing I could arrest him on. I could ask people to keep an eye out for the car, but not to pull it over or do anything about it.

I needed to figure out a way to get him behind bars and out of our lives. Maybe if I could find the car, I could plant something in it. Get him sent to jail and away from Charlie and Theo for good. I wouldn't rest until he was out of their lives.

"I'm just worried about the situation with her ex." I shrugged.

"You can be worried about her situation with her ex without touching her," she teased. Alice could be nosy when she wanted to be.

"How was your date?" I asked in an attempt to change the subject. Her eyes widened.

"How did you know about–*Lottie*!" She shook her head. "It was a waste of time, I'm not ready for the dating pool just yet. He was a bit of an ass."

"Need me to beat him up?" She laughed.

"As an officer of the law, should you be offering to beat people up?"

"You're my sister. There isn't anything I wouldn't do for you." She grabbed my hand and smiled.

"You're a good guy, Eli. You deserve to be happy." Her eyes wandered over to Charlie and back at me. "If it helps, I'm pretty sure she likes you, too."

If it helps, I'm pretty sure she likes you, too.

I kind of got the feeling she liked you more than in just a friendly way.

Both of my siblings' words played around in my head as I looked down at my coffee. The more time I spent with Charlie, the more my feelings grew. But I was still hesitant to take it past that point.

No matter how much I wanted to, I don't know if I could be in a relationship with her. I didn't feel like I was good enough for a girl like Charlie.

"We're just friends. I just want to help her get out of this situation with her ex."

"They usually say that some of the best relationships are built on friendship first," she quipped, taking a sip from her coffee.

I didn't know how to explain my feelings further. I didn't feel good enough for Charlie, but at the same time, the thought of anyone else having her made my blood boil. I felt protective over her. Possessive, almost. I knew deep in my heart that I wanted her to be mine. Maybe I needed to figure out a way to make myself good enough for her, to be the man she deserved. First, I needed to deal with Adam. I wasn't going to let him stand in the way of her happiness.

Thirty-Three

I wanted to try as much as possible to put everything that was happening with Adam in the back of my mind. It wasn't easy, that was for sure. I hadn't seen his car again, but there was a chance it wasn't even his car in the first place. I was likely just being paranoid because of the text. He hadn't sent any more since then. Maybe he finally realised that it was time to let go, I could only hope.

Today was supposed to be a fun day between Alice and I. I'd been super excited about going dress shopping for the gala since I first found out about it. I don't remember the last time I went clothes shopping; I don't think I'd worn a nice dress like the ones we were looking at today since prom. I tried to dress pretty for Adam wherever possible, but it never seemed to be enough for him. *I* never seemed to be enough for him.

This time I wasn't looking at dresses to please anyone else. I would buy a dress because I liked how I looked in it, not because I thought he would like how I looked in it. His favourite dresses were the ones that felt skin-tight and hugged every part of me. I hated those dresses; I felt self-conscious like every flaw and bump in my body was on show. They were uncomfortable. I loved dresses that had a little give, a little flow and made me feel relaxed.

I met up with Alice at the day care after we'd both dropped the kids off. She looked hesitant as she approached me with a hug.

"How are you doing?" she asked as she pulled away.

"I've been better," I answered honestly. "I didn't sleep well last night. Kept thinking I was hearing things outside."

"I'm sorry, Lottie. Elijah filled me in a bit with what he knew. Maybe you should stay with one of us until this all blows over?"

"I wouldn't want to put anybody out," I said, shaking my head as we started walking towards her car. "The boys were kind enough to let me stay one night as it is. I don't want to push my luck with them."

"I don't think you could ever push your luck with Elijah." She laughed softly, opening her car door.

"What do you mean by that?"

"My brother likes to give the impression he's this hard guy, but he's a big softie when it comes to the people he cares about." She paused. "I can see how much he cares about you, Lottie." I took a minute to take in her words as I climbed into the passenger seat. I wanted to deny it, to pretend I didn't think he cared about me or Theo, but I couldn't.

Someone who didn't care about me wouldn't have gotten so upset over the fact that I didn't call him when I was in trouble. I also couldn't deny that I was starting to care about him, too.

The more time I spent with him, the more I cared. The more I wanted to make him smile or talk about things to help take some of the weight he was clearly holding on his shoulders. I wanted to help him like he was helping me.

"He's a good guy. We didn't exactly get off to the best start, but I think he's more than made up for it. I appreciate the help he's given me, the help you've all given me. You've really made us feel like one of you guys." I felt my voice shake on the last word. I meant every part of that; our fresh start for the most part had exceeded our expectations. All I had wanted when moving here was to get away from Adam. I hadn't expected that along the way we'd find a new family. I felt honoured to be close to the Weatherston family.

"One of us! One of us!" she chanted mockingly, but I could see her eyes welling with tears.

"You're the sister I always wanted. Poor Lucas spent many hours wearing dresses and makeup because I was desperate for a little sister instead." She half laughed and half cried as she spoke. We spent the next few minutes teary and attempting to pull ourselves together.

"Lottie! This is supposed to be a fun day, let's go shopping," she said, excitedly pulling away from the car park. According to Alice, the best places to shop for dresses were just outside of town. I was a little glad to be getting out of Rosehaven for a few hours. I wouldn't have to worry about running into Adam.

I was overwhelmed with the options as we entered the store. It was covered head to toe in dresses of all colours and styles.

"How on Earth are we going to figure out where to start?" I questioned Alice as we walked in.

"Well, what style do you like the to wear?" she asked mindlessly, looking through a rack near the front of the store.

"I like more flowy dresses, ones that are more forgiving."

"And what's your favourite colour?"

I thought for a second before responding. "Like a burgundy red." She grabbed my hand and pulled me over to a rack of red dresses.

"This is where we start," she beamed as she started looking excitedly through the dresses, pulling out her favourites. It felt like an out-of-body experience trying on some of these dresses. It was like living someone else's life. They were all ridiculously pretty, but none of the ones I tried on so far felt like me. I wanted to look nice, but I didn't want to look different. The next one I tried on was a burgundy dress with a light sparkle in the pattern and a sweetheart neckline. I admired myself in the mirror as I twirled before showing Alice.

"You look beautiful," Alice gasped, placing her hands on her face. "That is my favourite one so far!" she squealed. I had never felt so beautiful before in my entire life. Even with my hair messy and no makeup on, I felt amazing.

I giggled as I gave Alice another twirl.

"I think this is it!" I said excitedly. After taking the dress off we switched. It was Alice's turn to find her outfit, which surprisingly didn't take long.

"I've been eyeing this one up on the website for ages," she admitted. I pulled my purse out to pay for my dress and she swatted my hand away. "This one is on me."

"Alice, you can't do that. It's too much." She shook her head.

"Please let me do this," she said as she pulled her own purse out. "Before you came to town I was really struggling. I am in the middle of a divorce, moving back to my old town where I didn't feel like I knew anybody. Having you come to town has really turned things around for me and I am grateful for your friendship." She grabbed my hand and I pulled her into a hug.

"I'm really glad to have met you," I said as we parted. I relented and let her pay. I found myself feeling excited about what was to come. No matter what, we were going to have a good time on Friday. I could feel it.

I was still on cloud nine from our shopping trip the next day when I started my shift at the café. I was washing up some of the cups from the morning rush when I heard the jingle of the bell behind me. Turning around, my eyes widened with panic.

"Adam," I breathed.

"Hi, Lottie. Fancy seeing you here," he drawled. My stomach was in knots at the sight of him. He looked rough, tired, and angry. "I think you and I need to have a conversation, don't you think?"

"You shouldn't be here." I attempted to feel for my phone in my pocket. I needed to call Elijah. I felt around, but I couldn't find it. I suddenly remembered I'd left it in the kitchen. *Shit.* Panic threatened to overwhelm me.

"That's not how you're supposed to talk to customers, Lottie. Although, you were always a terrible waitress." His words stung more than then they should have. Gone were the days where he praised me, where he told me how great I was. Only the darker side of Adam seemed to remain now. Adam and I got so caught up in our exchange neither of us heard the bell ring as another customer entered the café.

Thirty-Four

Elijah

W alking into the café I knew immediately something was wrong. The look of fear washing over
Charlie made me see red. It was a fair assumption
that the man arguing with Charlie was Adam based on the
picture of him she showed me before. He looked rougher now,
like he hadn't slept. *Desperate.* My blood was boiling listening
to the way he spoke to her. I watched as he grabbed onto her
arm, stopping her from moving away from him.

"I don't like the way your hands are touching my girl; I'd take
them off, if I were you." Both Charlie and Adam's gazes shot
round to face me as I spoke. I was grateful to be in my uniform
and on my way to work, it was a slightly more intimidating
attire. A flood of relief was shown on Charlie's face when our
eyes met. It was short-lived when I saw Adam's grip tighten
on her arm as he shot me a hard stare. The harder he gripped
her, the angrier I got. He had no right to be touching her. He

didn't even deserve to be breathing the same air she was.

"Did I stutter?" I followed up. *"Take. Them. Off,"* I said through gritted teeth. I grabbed onto Adam's shoulder, twisting him round and forcing him to let go of her. Charlie quickly moved herself to my side.

I grabbed her waist instinctively, pulling her close to my side.

"If you don't mind, pal, *my* girlfriend and I are trying to have a private conversation," Adam said, gesturing to her. *She's not yours, she will never be yours again.* I took a breath, steadying myself before responding.

"*Your* girlfriend?" I asked, mockingly. "Not anymore," I growled. Adam pushed his fists into my chest, but I didn't move an inch. I stood my ground, keeping one arm on Charlie the whole time. She was safe now. I was here.

"I'm only going to warn you once," I said sternly. "Keep your hands off of what is *mine.*" I don't know what came over me, claiming Charlie as my own, but it felt like the right thing to do. If he thought she was mine, he might leave her alone, that he no longer had a chance to be with her. Besides, I wished she was mine. "You go near Charlie or Theo ever again and you will regret it."

"*Charlie?* Who the hell do you think you're talking to? *Lottie* is *mine.* Theo is *my son.* You don't know who you're dealing with. You don't know what I'm capable of," Adam spat back. My heart was pounding, but I kept my expression stern.

"No, but I know what *I* am capable of."

I kept my eyes focused on his as I watched his reaction. The man who previously seemed to be in control of the situation was crumbling before me. I was in control here.

He looked at Charlie. I wanted to grab his face and force

him to look away. He didn't even deserve to look at her.

"Are you fucking serious, Lottie? *This* is who you left me for? We all know that uniform is an overcompensation for something," he spat at my feet. I didn't give him the satisfaction of any reaction, my face remaining stoic. "What is it for you, were you bullied in high school or something? Maybe you've got Daddy issues?" He laughed. *I saw red.* I grabbed his shirt and shoved him against the counter. Holding one of my arms to his neck I pinned him against it.

"You will *never* hurt her again." My voice was harsh as I spoke. "You don't even deserve to breathe the same air as her, do you understand me?" He gave no response. "If I were you, I'd crawl back to whatever hole you came out of and not come back." I pulled him back and threw him towards the door.

He looked between Charlie and I before kicking a chair across the room. He paused just before he left the café.

"This isn't over, Lottie. Your little boyfriend won't be there to save you next time." With that, he slammed the door behind him.

I felt the tension easing off my shoulders slightly as I watched him walk away, but my stomach was a mess. I couldn't bear the thought of someone hurting her or Theo. I didn't let go of Charlie; if anything, I pulled her closer to me. She accepted this and leant into me.

"I'm sorry, I couldn't find my phone. It all happened so fast," she said, panicked. I lifted her chin up to face me.

"It's okay, everything's okay," I whispered softly. "I told you I wasn't going to let anything happen to you, didn't I?" She nodded. She opened her mouth and then hesitated. "What's wrong?" I asked.

"Why were you acting like we were together?" She questioned. *Because I wished we were.*

"I wanted him to feel intimidated, to feel like you moved on and he'd lost you. Maybe he'd give up harassing you if he knew you had me protecting you." I gestured to my uniform.

"Oh...yeah, that makes sense." She pulled away from me slightly, giving me an empty feeling. "Good thinking." She brushed her hands on her apron. The silence was awkward as we both seemed to be racking our brains as to how to move on from what just happened. After a few beats, I spoke.

"I want you to come to the gala with me." I hesitated. "In case he shows up there. If he sees you as my date, then hopefully he'll back off."

"So, we'd be fake dating for the night?" The word *fake* stung a little, but that was exactly what I was suggesting.

"Yeah, I mean we are both going anyway, so why not go together? He's going to try to get you alone, Charlie. I can't let that happen." I kept my voice level in an attempt to disguise my emotion.

"Okay," she replied shakily.

"Okay." I mused.

"Daines isn't going to the gala, I'll ask him to sit in with my ma and the kids to keep an eye on them, in case Adam shows up there." I knew Daines wouldn't say no. Theo was just as much at risk as Charlie.

"Thank you." She smiled and I felt some of the awkwardness lift slightly. "Thank you as well for getting rid of him. I don't know what I would have done if you hadn't showed up." I saw her let out a deep breath.

"I'm always here for you. Please keep your phone in your pocket, though," I teased lightly.

"You don't have to worry, I won't be making that mistake

again." She paused. "I'm going to ask your ma if I can stay with them for a few days until the gala." As much as I wished she would stay with me, I was glad she wasn't going to be on her own. I would ask the Chief to keep a patrol car going down that street until I knew Adam was no longer a threat. I'd patrol it myself if I had to.

Charlie made me a coffee and we said our goodbyes. Lucas and I would meet the girls at Ma's house Friday before the gala. I was suddenly aware that I needed to go shopping for a better suit. I was planning on wearing an old tux I'd had for years, but it wasn't good enough for a date with Charlie.

After arriving at work, I explained the situation to Daines. He agreed to sit with Ma and the kids, but also teased me about the concept.

"So, the two of you are going to *pretend to be dating* in case this guy shows up?" he questioned.

"Yeah, if he thinks she has moved on, he hopefully will leave her alone."

"Answer me this, young Elijah." He held up his hands. "Why did you not just ask her out on a *real date*?"

"Why would I do that?" I was slightly taken aback by his comment.

"Because you clearly like this girl?" *Why did everyone keep trying to point that out to me?*

"No, I don't. We're just friends," I replied sternly.

"Eli, I have eyes. I see the way yours light up when you talk about her. Hell, she's beautiful, I don't blame you. If I was twenty years younger, I'd—"

"Don't you dare finish that sentence," I growled.

"See! If you didn't like her, why are you so jealous?" He might have had a point, but I wasn't going to tell him that.

Thirty-Five

Charlotte

"I don't like the way your hands are touching my girl; I'd take them off, if I were you." Both mine and Adam's gazes shot to the voice coming from behind us. I was surprised to see Elijah there dressed in his uniform, I let out a breath at the sight of him. *My girl.* His words vibrated through me. Adam tightened his grip on my arm as he shot Elijah a hard stare. Everything that followed felt like a blur to me.

My heart leapt when Adam pushed his fists into Elijah's chest, but he didn't move an inch. Elijah was like a solid rock, making Adam's attempts look pathetic. *Mine. My Girl.* His words were swimming around my head. I was suddenly glad Elijah was holding onto me because his words were making my legs weak. My heart was pounding as I watched the two interact. I let out another breath when Adam stormed out. I had a feeling however that wouldn't be the last I'd see of him. Pulling myself into Elijah, I felt myself clinging onto him like he was a safety blanket. It took me a moment to come back down to Earth and realise that he had been referring to me as if we were together to Adam, so I questioned him. My heart sank at his explanation. It made sense and obviously I knew we weren't together, but it hurt all the same to watch the idea of us being together evaporate. His suggestion about the gala made sense and I'd be stupid not to agree to it. Adam wasn't a small guy, but Elijah was bigger and far more intimidating. It made sense for me to keep close to him until we knew Adam was gone out of our lives for good.

Part of me wanted to pull out of the gala all together. The thought of leaving Theo scared me. Knowing Officer Daines was going to be there helped slightly, but I still wasn't convinced. I'd been really looking forward to this gala, but it felt a little bit wrong now. I wasn't sure if I'd even be able to let go and have fun now. It wasn't long till Elijah left and I was alone with my thoughts. I felt myself in a daze for the rest of my shift. Jane had tried to insist I go home but I didn't want to. I wanted to be where there were lots of people around, just in case. I had texted Lucy to ask if we could stay for a couple of days and received an immediate yes in response. I was grateful to not have to go back to my place alone.

Walking back to my car I couldn't help but feel paranoid at every step I took.

I kept looking behind me, expecting Adam to jump out at any moment. I couldn't pretend now that he wasn't here, that he wasn't really coming for me. I knew better than that. I managed to pick up Theo and get to the Weatherston house without any issues, but I felt sick the whole way. I pretended everything was okay for Theo and put on the happiest voice I could muster when asking him about his day. I had no intentions of filling him in on what was going on; it would only confuse and frighten him. We pulled up to the house and Lucy immediately opened the door.

"Don't worry, I've been filled in about everything," Lucy said, pulling me into a warm embrace. I wondered if it was Elijah or Alice who had filled her in. I was conscious not to let my emotions overwhelm me because I didn't want Theo to catch on. "I thought we could get a nice takeout for dinner?" She bounced this question between Theo and I. He seemed ecstatic at the thought.

"Thank you, that's a brilliant idea. My treat, though," I added and she looked intently at me. I imagined we would get into a further debate about this shortly. For now, though I was happy to be here, I felt safer here than my own place and Theo had Violet to play with. For just a moment, I allowed myself to pretend everything was normal.

* * *

I didn't see Adam at all in the next few days, but I felt him. I felt like he was watching my every move. I walked along, constantly turning my head. Elijah checked in on me every day, sometimes twice a day, especially when I was working. He seemed to make a point of coming in regardless of whether he was on shift. It felt a bit like I had my own personal bodyguard, it helped me feel slightly safer. I also got texts from Lucas who had clearly been filled in on the situation, as well. I was grateful for the support, it made it better knowing that people had my back. I don't remember the last time I felt like someone had my back and now there were multiple people.

Elijah had told me he organised a patrol car to go down his mother's street at night and it helped me relax more in the evenings. I enjoyed the small talk with Alice and Lucy. I watched the kids playing and Theo laughing, having no idea what was really happening. That his father was stalking us and could attack at any minute. He was free from the anxiety of it all and that is exactly where I wanted him to be. This had all been for him.

I couldn't believe the gala had come round so quickly and felt a buzz of excitement all day. Alice and Lucy had convinced me that it would indeed be fun and I was definitely going. I had never been particularly good at makeup, so Alice did it for me as we were getting ready. I spent a lot of time adding soft curls to my hair.

I felt beautiful. I felt unstoppable.

It was surreal to put the dress on again, and despite everything that was going on, I still felt amazing. I was nervous about my fake date with Elijah. We hadn't established any rules and I wasn't exactly sure what it all meant. I regretted not discussing boundaries with him beforehand. Should we dance together? Should I hold his hand as we walk in? Am I supposed to kiss him? If we were really boyfriend and girlfriend, there would be affection and kissing. That's a pretty normal thing to do. My heart raced at the thought of kissing Elijah. I couldn't stop the nervous butterflies in my stomach. I was completely and entirely out of my element here.

Walking down the stairs with Alice I was greeted by Lucy and Daines at the bottom. "Don't you two just look beautiful!" Lucy gasped. Daines smiled at me. I didn't know him well, but I knew he was close with Elijah. That in itself wasn't an easy feat, so he must have been special. The doorbell rang and

Lucy rushed to answer it. I heard her complimenting both the boys as they entered. Elijah came through first with a bunch of roses in his hands. *My favourites.* Did he know that or was it just a coincidence?

He looked unbearably handsome in his tux and I felt my cheeks go red just looking at him. Tall, dark and handsome was the description fictional books would give him and here I was, getting to go on a date with him. Albeit, a fake one.

"You look gorgeous, Charlie," he said, handing me the bunch of flowers. My cheeks flushed as I felt all the eyes in the room on me. Alice cleared her throat behind me. "You look okay, I guess." He smirked as he addressed his sister. She smacked him on the shoulder as she walked past him.

"Meter is running folks, we better get going," Lucas said as he walked into the room.

"Don't do anything I wouldn't," Daines said, winking at Elijah as we made our way out of the house after Lucy made us all take a picture together. Elijah wrapped his arm around my waist for the photo. The bright smile on my face in the picture was nothing but genuine. Alice and Lucas walked towards the cab ahead of us and Elijah slipped his hand into mine. We weren't at the gala yet, so I felt unsure as to why he was starting already. Maybe he wanted to get into the moment early? I looked back at the house, a sudden anxious wave hitting me as I remembered I was leaving Theo alone.

"Do you trust Daines?" I asked, turning back to face him.

"With my life," Elijah said confidently, giving me all the reassurance I needed.

Thirty-Six

Elijah

I had never had much interest in going to the gala, but I'd also never gotten to go to it with a beautiful woman before. I felt sick all morning, suddenly anxious that this was all a terrible idea and maybe I should back out. I tried to go for a run to calm myself down, but it was no use. Not even the piano was saving me today. I watched the time pass all day, pacing around the house. Everything in me wanted tonight to go well, *needed* it to. Despite the fact that this was all supposed to be fake, I felt this immense pressure building inside of me.

It was finally time to get ready and I fussed over my tux for over an hour. I had bought it the other day. Lucas reassured me it was good, but I still felt self-conscious.

"Cabs here," Lucas called out. I finally had to stop fussing and accept that this was as good as it was going to get. I picked up the bunch of roses I'd bought her earlier off the side. I'd remembered her telling Violet that they were her favourite. I didn't know which colour she liked best, so I got a variety. I suddenly felt a sense of regret; this was a fake date, after all. Should I even be buying her flowers?

"You are such a softie," Lucas teased as he eyed up the roses. "If you buy Lottie flowers when she's your fake girlfriend, I wonder what you'd get her if she was your real one?"

Everything. I'd get her everything she wanted.

I ignored his teasing as we climbed into the cab, making our way over to my mother's house first.

Lucas spent the ride wittering on about various sports fixtures, but I could barely concentrate on the conversation. I had to concentrate instead on trying not to throw up as we got closer and closer.

I nearly collapsed on the spot when I saw her standing at the bottom of the stairs. My heart was in my throat as I looked at her. She was beautiful. She was everything. And tonight, she was mine. There was a slight awkward tension in the room as I greeted and gave the flowers to Charlie. My family was acting like they were watching a show.

It felt natural to slip my hand into hers as we walked out of the house, I didn't think about it as I did it.

I just knew I wanted to touch her and before I knew it, we were holding hands. I sensed her nervousness about leaving Theo and tried to reassure her, promising that we would have a great night.

There was a buzz in the cab as we made our way to the venue. Lucas had taken the front seat and Charlie was sitting in between Alice and I. Our legs touched together with the movement of the car and I found myself reaching my hand onto her leg, once again not even thinking. She moved her hand on top of mine. We didn't acknowledge this touch verbally, but it felt right. Everything about having her close to me felt right.

Upon arrival I watched as her eyes lit up, looking around the venue. I didn't care what the venue looked like; I already knew it was nowhere near as beautiful as she was right now.

We found a table and Lucas got the first round of drinks. Charlie held hers in the air.

"To fresh starts," she beamed.

"To fresh starts," we all mused, clinking our glasses together. After a few drinks, Lucas and Alice left to wander around and mingle, leaving Charlie and I alone.

"Will you dance with me?" she asked sweetly. My stomach dropped. I hated dancing, but for some reason, the prospect of dancing with her excited me.

"Of course." I stood up, grabbing her hand and leading her onto the dance floor. I fumbled slightly at first, my nerves getting the better of me. However, I soon found control of myself and lead her round the dance floor, one hand on her arm and the other low down on her back. Out of the corner of my eye I saw Taylor staring us down and I smirked. I liked him knowing that she came with me, that she was mine for the night. We didn't talk whilst we danced, but we held continuous eye contact as we moved around. She smiled as we glided and laughed when I spun her. Soon the rest of the room faded away from my mind and it was just the two of us. I almost forgot that all of this was supposed to be fake, it certainly didn't feel that way for me. We danced for a few more songs before reluctantly stopping for a drink break. She didn't let go of my hand as she led me back towards a table.

Soon after, Lucas found his way to us as the music turned more upbeat now.

"Mind if I borrow your date for a dance?" he asked, looking at me.

"Not at all." I smiled softly. Charlie smiled at me before she grabbed Lucas' hand and walked towards the dance floor with him.

I watched as Lucas and Charlie danced together on the floor, him playfully spinning her round until she was so dizzy that they both laughed. If this was anyone other than my brother, jealously would be consuming me right now. I'd be ripping her away from them and taking her back into my arms in a heartbeat. I knew she was safe with Lucas, he cared for her like she was a sister. Despite the fact I hadn't admitted it, he also knew the feelings I had for her. He enjoyed teasing me, but he would never go over that line.

I felt my shoulders relax and I couldn't help but smile as I watched them. I felt a presence at my side and turned to see Alice next to me.

"I'm surprised you're allowing him to dance with your girl."

"She's not my—" I cut myself off. The fact she wasn't actually my girl stung. That none of this was real. For one night I wasn't going to deny it. I was happy pretending she was mine because I wished she was. "Lucas is harmless." She nodded at my words.

"He's always been the life of the party, eh?" She wasn't wrong there. My brother was always the fun one, always a joy to have around. "We can't let them have all the fun though, can we?" She smiled up at me before grabbing my hand and pulling me onto the dance floor. Before I knew it, I was surrounded by Charlie and my siblings dancing, smiles and laughter flowing through the group effortlessly. I smiled and laughed, too, surrounded by three of my favourite people in the whole world. In this moment, I didn't feel like I needed to look over my shoulder, that I wasn't in control. My breath was steady and my body was calm. I relaxed and enjoyed every second, periodically spinning Alice and Charlie around. Any moment I could, I pulled Charlie close to me; my hand grazing her back or holding her hand. At first, I was worried that she would be annoyed or upset by my touch, but it soon became clear she wasn't. My hand would touch hers and she would grab it back, giving it a gentle squeeze. When I would pull her close, she would lean into me. My hand would touch her back and she would look at me and smile. Every single time we touched it felt electric to me. Her presence was exhilarating and calming to me at the same time, I wanted to feel this way every single day. This was the happiest night of my entire life.

The rest of the evening was a mixture of dancing, laughing, and talking. We occasionally took a break from the dance floor and Charlie and I would just talk. We avoided the looming situation of Adam and turned the conversation to more positive memories. She talked about her love for music and how she missed going running. I told her about all the running routes locally with a promise we would go running together soon; that I would show her all the best places to go. She then talked more to me about her grandpa. There was a fondness in her expression as she spoke of him. It was clear how much he meant to her; he was the one who gave her that love for music. It made me want to play for her again. I would play for her every day if she let me. The way she looked at me was addicting. Making her smile was like a drug to me and I never wanted that feeling to stop. I didn't want to come down from the high that was being with Charlie.

Lucas and Alice called it a night before us, but I just wasn't ready for it to end. I could tell Charlie felt the same as she made no attempt to leave with them. We sat down on an empty table and continued to talk until last calls were given and the gala was winding down. Our bodies getting closer with each moment, my hand grazing her knee and hers lingering on my thigh. Knowing this night was shortly going to end was paining me, but eventually we stood making our way to wait for a cab outside.

"I had the best time tonight; I genuinely don't remember the last time I had that much fun," she said, breaking the silence.

"Me, too," I mused. "I actually don't think I've ever had that much fun." We stood on the sidewalk together; I was facing out into the car park whilst she was facing me. Out of the corner of my eye I spotted a figure lurking, knowing immediately it was Adam.

"Is it bad I am already excited about next year?" she asked, blissfully unaware of who was behind her. I caught his eye and felt the anger rising in my chest. Without thinking I placed my hand on her face and pulled her lips to mine.

Thirty-Seven

Charlotte

The gala was incredible.

Truthfully, I hadn't been expecting much given the fact this was a small town. I was wrong; Rosehaven went all out. This was clearly the big event of the year. I don't know how I suddenly got the confidence to ask Elijah to dance, but it just felt right. We had been exchanging stolen touches throughout the night so far, but I didn't feel like hiding them anymore. I was more than happy to be seen by his side that night. I could feel his nerves when we first started dancing, but we seemed to settle into a rhythm.

His touch was warm and I couldn't help but study every feature of his face. Nobody would deny that Elijah was attractive, but the way his features softened when he looked at me made my stomach drop. It felt like he was showing me parts of him that were a secret, that I was the only one he was letting in. He made me feel special.

I tried to rationalise in my brain that all of this was fake, that he was putting on a show in case Adam was watching. I'd looked everywhere since we got here and there was no sign of Adam—except a tense moment when I caught Daniel staring at us dancing. Truthfully, though, none of this felt fake. Every moment with Elijah felt completely natural, that this was just a real date.

When he grabbed my hand or touched my leg, it didn't feel like he was overthinking it. It felt like he was doing it because he wanted to. I knew I was reciprocating because I wanted to, not because I felt like I had to. After a short break, I found myself back on the dance floor with Lucas. You could definitely tell Lucas was the youngest child by the way he behaved, always teasing and laughing.

"I hope my brother is being the perfect gentleman for you?" he asked as he spun me around.

"He is." I looked over at Elijah, watching us. "He is the perfect gentleman." My eyes met with Lucas again and he smiled widely at me. He bit his lip and I could tell there was something he wanted to say.

"He's been a lot happier since you came to town, you know?" He continued dancing independently as he spoke. The classical music had seemingly turned into a DJ set in the latter half of the evening. "He really cares about you." Lucas kept side eyeing his brother, as if worried we would be overhead.

"I really care about him, too." Lucas smiled, looking relieved to have gotten that off of his chest as we continued to dance. I felt a sense of relieve admitting that, too.

Before long, Alice and Elijah wandered over to the join us on the dance floor, Elijah taking his place next to me. I don't know how long we all danced together, but it felt like it was going too quickly. I wanted to live in this moment for hours, to be with these people for hours. My people. I was happy here, I was safe. What I enjoyed the most about the evening was just getting to sit and talk to Elijah, to get to know him better. No topic seemed to be off limits between us. I was disappointed when we had to leave, I didn't feel ready to go. We walked side by side as we went outside to wait for a cab. We were facing each other and I felt this desire to reach out to him, but I held back.

"I had the best time tonight; I genuinely don't remember the last time I had that much fun."

"Me, too," he responded. "I actually don't think I've ever had that much fun." His words made my heart soar, it was nice to be on the same page.

"Is it bad I am already excited about next year?" I felt like the question was slightly lame and was worried he would find it needy. Before I could speak again, his hands were on my face and his lips were on mine. I felt myself melt into the kiss. He moved one of his hands to my hips, gripping me tightly. It took me by surprise, but my mouth was soon following his. We stayed locked for a moment before he pulled away and looked behind me. I swung my head round to see what he was looking at and noticed Adam in the other side of the car park.

My heart sank for brief moment. I thought he had been kissing me because he wanted to. Now I realised it was part of the show. Because that's all that this is, a show. We both watched as Adam turned and stormed away. I couldn't bring myself to meet Elijah's gaze again.

I felt foolish for even thinking he wanted me in that way.

"I can't believe he would even show up here," Elijah said, shaking his head. Despite the fact we had pulled apart, his hand still lingered on my hip, causing me to shiver. "Are you cold?" He immediately started taking his jacket off and handed it to me. My brain was spinning all over the place as I put his jacket on. One minute I thought he was just doing this to keep Adam away and the next minute I felt like he was doing this because he wanted to. I was struggling to figure out where I stood. Maybe the situation was just too messy for us to move onto anything more. After I put the jacket on, he pulled me into him to keep me warm. Despite my mental turmoil, I didn't fight it. When this night ended, we were likely no longer going to be fake dating anymore and these moments of closeness would cease to exist. I could still taste him on my lips as I leaned my head into the chest. I heard the cab pull up moments later and went to move away, but he still held onto me.

"Elijah, the cab's here," I said, looking up at him.

"I know, I just wanted to hold you close for another minute before this is all over." There was a sadness in his tone as he relented and let go of me. He opened the door for me to enter the cab. I couldn't help thinking, if neither of us wanted this to end, where did we go from here?

Thirty-Eight

Elijah

When I finally got home after I made sure Charlie got in safely, I crashed hard with thoughts of our kiss. I would be lying if I said I didn't enjoy the look on Adam's face after I kissed her. I would also be lying if I said I only kissed her because he was watching. Truthfully, I had been gearing myself up to kiss her the whole night. It was seeing Adam that finally gave me the motivation to do it. Even after he was gone, I was desperate to keep her close. I wanted to kiss her again, but I felt like I didn't have a good reason to. That she would push me away when she realised Adam was gone. But she hadn't known he was there when we kissed, had she? I couldn't help but notice that her gaze lowered after our kiss. I sat in my regret for a while, wishing I had done more, said more to her. Wishing I had told her how I felt, that this was all real for me. When I held onto her as the car arrived, it was because I was terrified to let her go. I was worried that once the night was over and tomorrow came, we would go back to being just friends. I didn't want to just be friends with Charlie. I wanted nights like tonight, over and over again.

I woke the next morning to the sound of my phone ringing. Turning it over, I realised it was almost 10:00 a.m. I'm not sure the last time I slept that late. I looked at the caller ID and saw Daines was ringing.

"Morning," I said groggily into the phone.

"Oh, no. Did I wake you up after your big night?" He chuckled, sounding far too preppy for the morning.

"What do you want, Daines?"

"Okay, okay. Straight to business, I guess. I just wanted to let you know I never saw Adam last night and I wanted to ask how your night went."

"I saw him, he was outside the gala as we were leaving. I wondered if he was trying to catch her in a vulnerable position at the end of the night."

"Most likely, he probably wasn't expecting you to be there. What did you do when you saw him?" *I kissed her.* The words were on the tip of my tongue, but I didn't speak. "Elijah, what did you do?" Daines asked again.

"I kissed her." My words were met with a surprised laugh from the other end of the phone.

"You have some balls, Elijah Weatherston, I'll give you that. Girl's ex is staring straight at you so your response is to kiss her." He laughed harder. I paused whilst he caught his breath.

"I think I would have kissed her either way." I'm not sure why I admitted that to him.

"So where do you two go from here?"

"I'm not sure." I knew where *I* wanted to go from here, but I still wasn't sure exactly how she felt about me. The phone call ended shortly after and I was left staring at the ceiling. A little while later I pulled out my phone again and realised I'd missed a text from Charlie.

Charlie: Thank you for last night. It felt nice to let loose again and forget about everything.

I wasn't expecting her to reach out and it felt like the wind was knocked out of me. I quickly fired back.

Elijah: Same time next year?

It was a slightly lame response and there was a lot more I needed to say to her, but over text was not the way to go about it. I'd find a reason to see her in the next couple of days.

The next day I was back at work. I avoided going into the café as I didn't want that to be the first time I saw Charlie after the gala. I made a note to text her today to arrange a time to meet up. I was subjected to minor roasting from Daines when I arrived at work. He had written Elijah and Charlotte in a love heart using the dirt on the car. *Real mature.* Lucas had already spent yesterday giving me the third degree about it all, as well. I seemed to be talking with everyone but Charlie about it all.

A couple hours later, a call came over the radio.

"Aggressive male at Little Town's Day Care." My heart sank. That was the day care Violet and Theo went to. Daines blasted the sirens and we headed straight there. As we entered the foyer, we could hear a man shouting. The voice was eerily familiar to me. Looking up, I spotted Adam yelling at one of the staff members. He turned to watch us come in with a loud groan leaving his lips when he realised it was me.

"I'm pretty sure I told you to stay away from Charlie and Theo." I felt Daines tensing next to me, readying himself for response.

"I'm just here to pick up my son." Adam seemed to lower his voice in our presence, but it was still layered with tension.

"I told you, sir, you do not have permission to do that. You are not on the approved list," the worker calmly tried to explain.

"He's my son!" Adam's voice was raised again.

Theo appeared from behind the desk. The lady gave me a sad look, making me realise he'd be there this whole time Adam was yelling. Theo spotted me across the room and ran behind my legs, gripping them tightly.

"Please don't make me go with him." His voice was hushed as I bent down to his face level. I could see he'd been crying and tears threatened to fall on his face again.

"Don't worry, buddy. You aren't going anywhere with him, I promise." Theo gave a soft smile.

"How dare you speak to my son!" Adam was yelling again and I quickly stood back up on my feet, pushing Theo lightly behind me again. "Theo, we are going. *Now*." His tone made my blood boil. If this was how he spoke to a child, *his child,* I dreaded to think how he spoke to Charlie.

"He's not going anywhere with you," I growled. "Charlie and Theo are part of my family now and I won't let you anywhere near them." Adam approached me and Daines pulled Theo further away. We were face-to-face now, both of us seething with anger.

"They're my family," he spat.

"You don't deserve them." My tone matched his now. It took

all of my self-control not to launch myself at him. "Charlie deserves better than some asshole who gets his kicks out of scaring children and beating defenceless women." Adam launched himself at me, but I was one step ahead. I grabbed his arms and shoved him to the floor, pulling the cuffs out of my belt and slapping them on him. I leaned close into his ear. "If you ever come near my family again, getting arrested will be the least of your worries." I picked him off the ground with force. Officers Taylor and Lawrence, who had arrived for back up, stepped in as I passed Adam over. I expected Taylor to give me flack since we last saw each other at the gala, but there was nothing but anger towards Adam as he apprehended him. He may take a while to come to terms with the fact Charlie is mine, but we can at least agree upon her ex.

"Throw away the key on that one," Daines said sternly as he followed them out to get him loaded in. I turned my attention to Theo who had run into my arms. I picked him up and held him tightly to my chest.

"Is he gone now?" he asked through tears.

"He is, the other officers are taking him away now."

"Will you stay with me?" he pleaded. "I want Mommy," he sobbed.

"I'm not going anywhere, buddy. I'm staying right here with you until your mommy gets here, okay?" The workers had already called Charlie. Although they struggled to reach her at first, I gathered she was now on her way. I took Theo into one of the spare playrooms to help him calm down. Despite all the mistakes I had made in my life. I could protect him and Charlie. I could keep them safe. We played cars until I heard Charlie burst through the door, running straight to him and taking her in his arms.

"Theo, are you okay?" She was breathless as she spoke with tears streaming down her face. He nodded.

"I'm okay. Elijah stopped Daddy from taking me." She looked up at me with a teary smile.

Thirty-Nine

Charlotte

L ooking at my phone I realised I had two missed calls from Theo's day care.

"Jane, do you mind if I call them back?" She nodded and I ran outside to make the call. My hand immediately went over my mouth as they explained what was happening. I ran back inside.

"Adam's trying to take him," I said, the panic clear in my voice. Jane ushered me out the door without another word. I was only down the block from the day care and I ran as fast as my legs would take me. I wasn't going to let him get to my boy, I wasn't going to let him hurt him. Every punch, slap and kick I had taken had been to prevent him from hurting Theo, and he wasn't going to start now. He wasn't going to get near him as long as I still lived. I was out of breath when I arrived and saw Adam sitting in a police car outside of the day care. I took a breath of relief when I realised he didn't have him, he hadn't gotten away with it. Daines caught my eye as I approached.

"Theo's okay, he's inside with Eli." He smiled softly. Theo was okay, Elijah was with him. Elijah would never let anything happen to him. As I approached, I caught sight of them playing through the glass and my chest swelled. I burst through the door and ran straight to Theo, overwhelmed with relief that he was okay.

"Theo, are you okay?" I needed to know for certain and he nodded.

"I'm okay. Elijah stopped Daddy from taking me." Tears filled my eyes again as I looked at Elijah. He had promised me he wouldn't let anything happen and he meant it. I planted kisses all over Theo's face, causing him to laugh and try to squirm out of my grip. Elijah was smiling, too, as he watched.

"Why don't I take you two back to my place for a bit?" he asked. I turned to him and nodded. He went outside to talk to Daines whilst we collected Theo's stuff together.

"Daines is going to ride with the others to get Adam booked in and charged," he said as he came back in to get us. "So, you two get to ride in my cruiser." Theo's eyes lit up at the thought of this.

"Can I turn the siren on?" he asked excitedly.

"When we get back, yeah, of course. Not in town, though." Elijah smiled widely. "Ready to go?" We followed him out into the street as Theo and I both climbed into the backseat. I wasn't ready to be apart from him yet. When we arrived at Elijah's place, he let Theo climb in the front to turn the sirens on. The traumatic events of earlier seemed to be far from Theo's mind now.

"Can I watch TV?" Theo asked as we got inside. I looked to Elijah for his approval, considering we were in his house, and he gave a small nod.

"Of course." I wanted a moment alone with Elijah, anyway. We hadn't properly spoken since we kissed at the gala and now there was the added situation of today to be discussed. After Theo was settled, I found myself in the familiar place that was Elijah's arms as we embraced.

"Thank you for everything you did today," I said, burying my face in his chest.

"We don't have to sort anything out now, but it would be worth using this to get a restraining order for both of you against him. Now that he's in custody, it should be fairly straight forward." I agreed with him, it was something I should have done a long time ago. I couldn't have another event like today happen again. I needed to protect Theo. We pulled away from each other and I found my eyes lingering on Theo.

"I can't help but feel like all of this is my fault."

"Don't you dare, Charlie; this isn't your fault. None of it is."

"I don't know what we would have done without you, Elijah." I turned my gaze to him. "I know the whole fake dating thing wasn't exactly something you wanted to do."

"It wasn't." My heart sank. *Of course, it wasn't something he wanted to do. He just felt bad for the woman with nothing, who can barely keep her child safe. I'm just his duty.*

"I'd have preferred it if it had all been real." His eyes now avoided mine.

"Was any of it real for you?" I lifted his chin with my finger.

"Every single minute of it." We both froze for a moment as the weight of what had been said lingered. I lifted myself up on my toes and met his lips with mine. This time there was no confusion, no unspoken words.

We both knew that we wanted this. He briefly pulled away,

eyeing Theo to make sure he was distracted, before pushing me up against the wall. His lips crashed hard against mine as my back pressed into the wall. His hands moved to my hips gripping me with urgency, like he was afraid he would lose me. I wanted more, I needed more. We broke apart and he ran his hand through his beard before smiling.

"Does this mean I can take you for a proper date tomorrow?" he teased. "Maybe the three of us could go out for a picnic or something." His hands lingered on my hips and I suddenly found myself missing the taste of him.

"I'd really like that." I ran my hand through his hair.

"I really hate to say this, but I need to get back to work." He sighed. "Will you guys be okay here until I get back? There is some cash if you want to order takeout and Lucas should be home soon."

"We'll be okay. What time will you be back?"

"Around eight," he said, still making no attempt to move. He leaned his forehead against mine. "I really don't want to go." I laughed at his words as he placed a kiss on my forehead. "If they hadn't already seen me today, I'd definitely be calling in sick."

"Adam is being locked up as we speak, we're safe. You don't need to worry about us anymore."

"I am always going to worry about the two of you. I just want to make you happy."

"Well, you're doing a pretty good job of it so far." He scoffed and kissed me again.

I could get used to this feeling, the feeling of being his. It was another twenty minutes before we finally broke apart and he was back out the door. Theo and I watched him leaving out the window, waving at him as he drove away.

I couldn't help but feel a sense of emptiness now that he was gone, but also excitement about our official date tomorrow. I felt like a weight had been lifted off my shoulders now that Adam had been arrested. There was no longer someone lurking in every corner. I was free to move on with my life and I wanted to move on together with Elijah.

Forty

Elijah

It felt like a fire had been lit inside me when Charlie kissed me. Everything I had been wanting and thinking about over the past few weeks was finally coming true. If Theo hadn't been in the same room, I wasn't sure if I'd have been able to control myself. I wanted more and I certainly didn't want to leave. I thought about her the entire way back to the police station. I thought about our date tomorrow. I thought about everything I wanted to do now that Adam was out of the way. Upon arrival, I found Daines standing in the foyer.

"He's all tucked in his cell nicely," he reassured me. "How's Lottie and Theo?" I still enjoyed being the only person to call her Charlie. Despite the fact I constantly referred to her as Charlie, nobody else used it. It made me feel special, like what we had was different. I would be lying if I said I didn't enjoy how it flustered Adam, too.

"They are good, I dropped them off at my place." I hesitated, suddenly having a strong urge to tell Daines more. "I'm taking her out tomorrow."

"Is this fake date thing not redundant now we arrested him?" He raised an eyebrow.

"For real this time," I explained and he slapped me on the back.

"Good for you, Eli! I knew you'd finally come round to admitting you liked her," he said, teasingly. It wasn't often I opened up, but it felt good to talk about everything. To not be completely closed off to everything. If I wanted to be good enough for Charlie, then I needed to be more open. I was determined to be the man she deserved.

We stayed fairly close to the station for the rest of the shift. I was nervous that Adam would suddenly jail break. I knew it was slightly irrational, but I wanted to be nearby just in case. Things were finally starting to look up and I wasn't going to have him ruin it.

When I got home, I found Lucas, Theo, and Charlie on the couch watching a movie. It felt good to be home, it felt good to have them here.

"We saved you some pizza," Lucas said as I sat myself down next to Charlie, my hand immediately finding its way to her thigh. I saw Lucas's eyebrow raise, but he didn't say anything. We all sat there and chatted all evening.

Well, at least the adults did. Theo didn't make it to the end of the movie before he passed out. Charlie cuddled into me whilst we watched the movie and it felt nice to have her close.

I found myself fantasising about what it would be like if this was our life. What would happen if they moved in one day and we got to spend our evenings cooking together, watching TV. Maybe on the weekends we would go for family walks. I knew

I was getting ahead of myself, but I couldn't help it. I wanted a life with Charlie more than I ever had wanted anything before. After watching a second movie we decided to call it a night.

"You guys are welcome to take my room again. Do you want me to carry him up?"

"You don't have to sleep on the couch. I'm happy if you wanted to come share with us," She rocked back and forth on her heels. "No funny business, obviously."

"Oh, I wouldn't." I held my hands up defensively. I'd like to think I was more of a gentleman than that. I didn't want to rush anything with her. I wanted to savour everything.

"I know, I just wanted to make sure we were on the same page."

"Only if you're sure. I'm happy on the couch," I offered.

"I'm sure, Elijah." She smiled sweetly at me. I hesitated for a minute, giving her time to change her mind, but she didn't. Picking Theo up, I followed her up the stairs. It was a strange sense of déjà vu, only this time, I wouldn't be leaving. I tucked Theo into the left side of the bed whilst Charlie went into the bathroom to change before climbing into the middle of the bed. I went into the bathroom after looking at myself in the mirror. I found myself smiling at my own reflection. Every moment seemed to feel surreal. Keeping on my sweats, I took off my shirt and climbed into the bed next to Charlie. I was quiet for a minute, half expecting her to ask me to leave, but she didn't. I wrapped my arms around her and she turned to face me, planting a soft kiss on my lips.

"I don't usually get into bed with a man before our first date," she said quietly.

"Technically it's our second, if you count the gala," I corrected.

"Of course. How could I forget about our first date." She laughed softly. "I was worried you only kissed me because Adam was watching…"

Elijah, you idiot. "I've been desperate to kiss you since we sat outside in the backyard at Ma's place. I did it because I wanted to, not because of anyone or anything else." I kissed her again, more tenderly this time. Her arms made their way around my neck.

"I hope you regret being mean to me that first time I came into town," she joked.

"Well, in my defence, you failed to stop for a police officer." She hit me playfully. "Of course, I regret it. I am really sorry about that, I was having a bad day."

"Why was that again?" she asked her hands running along my chest.

"A couple of kids got away from me earlier in the day. I get really frustrated when I make stupid mistakes, it makes me anxious. When my dad died, I chased down the guy who shot him. He got away, too. I blame myself for it and I can't stand it when I fail." I was surprised by how easily that admission came out.

"Oh, Eli," she whispered. "It's not your fault, you were only fifteen."

"It was my fau—"

"No, it was never your fault, not for a minute," she cut me off, her whisper sterner now. "You spent all this time taking care of everyone else and no one was looking after you." She kissed me then and I returned it eagerly. "I'm here now, I promise I will look after you just as well as you do me." We settled down in the bed silently after that. I fell into an uncharacteristically deep sleep that night.

Elijah

Everything was better when she was near me.

Forty-One

Charlotte

⟡

My heart ached for Elijah after our conversation the previous night. He had clearly been carrying the guilt of his father's death around with him all these years. I finally felt like all the puzzle pieces were coming together and I was starting to understand him better. I woke up the next morning safe in his arms as Theo woke up shortly after and pounced on me. How this kid had so much energy in the morning was beyond me.

"Morning," a groggy Elijah said next to me as Theo threw himself on top of him. "Did your Mommy not teach you that it's impolite to jump on people right after they wake up?" he asked tickling Theo.

"Sorry, I guess I forgot that lesson," I said with a yawn.

"What's for breakfast?" This kid was unbelievable.

Elijah smirked and raised his eyebrow at me. "Pancakes?"

"I think it might be better if I make them this morning," I

said, making my way out of bed. Theo jumped again toward Elijah, but this time he was more prepared, grabbing him and tossing him in the air, enticing squeals from Theo. I had a feeling I was going to get used to this chaos and that I was going to love it.

After breakfast we discussed our plans for the day. "I figured maybe we could pack a picnic and head up to the creek. There's a playground nearby for Theo."

I loved the fact he was including Theo in this and had genuinely thought about how to make it fun for everyone. A few hours later, we stopped off at my place to grab a couple days' worth of clothes, just in case. I didn't want to be assumptive, but at the same time, I knew I wanted to spend as much time with Elijah as possible. Heading up to the creek, I was taken aback with the views. I hadn't gotten to explore as much of this side of the town yet and it was beautiful. It looked exactly like all the pictures on my Google search before I picked this place. Theo immediately ran towards the playground. Elijah placed the blanket nearby and we sat down close together, watching him.

"I picked this town after a random Google search, did I tell you that?" Elijah shook his head. "I just wanted to find somewhere peaceful to go, I'm so glad I picked this place."

"I'm glad you picked this place, too." He smiled, moving closer to me as I rested my chin on my shoulder. "I don't know how I got so lucky to have you in my life." His voice was sincere as he spoke.

"You know I come as a package deal, right?" My eyes wandered to Theo.

I was nervous for Elijah's response. I know we had feelings for each other, but I couldn't blame him if he didn't want to take on a kid.

He could get any girl he wanted to; he didn't need to settle for one with baggage.

"I do." He nodded, his gaze following mine to Theo. "I feel like I've won the lottery with this package." I blushed at his words.

It always felt like Elijah knew exactly what to say to make me feel better. I had never felt this safe around someone before. Even in the early days with Adam, I found myself feeling insecure, but I never felt that way with Elijah. I cuddled tighter into him and he put his arm around my shoulder, pulling me close.

"Careful, you'll be stuck with us before you know it," I teased.

"I hope I'm stuck with the two of you forever," he said, planting a kiss on my forehead.

We ate our picnic talking about anything and everything. Elijah told Theo about how he used to come fishing here with his dad. I loved the fact that Elijah was talking about him with Theo; I knew how hard it was for him.

Theo begged Elijah to bring him fishing sometime and he promised he would. If I knew anything about Elijah's promises, he meant them. After his brief respite, Theo was back to exploring.

"Have you heard anything about Adam today?" I didn't want to ask, but I knew Elijah was being kept in the loop.

"He's still being kept at the station last I heard. They want to talk me through my statement tomorrow when I'm back on shift."

"Why do they need to talk you through it?"

"It's just procedure, nothing to worry about. They just want to make sure everything I say lines up right so they can charge him. They'll do the same with Daines' statement, too." We went quiet for a moment as I thought about Adam. I felt guilty that he was clouding my thoughts when I was supposed to be on a date with Elijah, but I couldn't get him off my brain. I was angry about how he treated me and everything he had put me through. I was frustrated that it took me so long to get away.

"He always made me feel like I was asking too much," I said, my thoughts finding their way out loud.

"You were never asking too much, Charlie; you were just asking the wrong person." He grabbed my hand. "Nothing you could ever ask me would be too much."

If that had been Adam saying that, I would know he was only saying it to make me forgive him for something he had done. Elijah was different. Elijah meant every single word he just said. I genuinely believed looking at him now that if I asked him, he would do anything for me. That thought excited me and terrified me at the same time.

This time it was me who initiated the kiss as I brought my free hand up to his face, bringing my lips to his. I found myself melting into him as he removed his hand from mine and placed it on my back, pulling me closer to him. I had spent so many days feeling like a burden, feeling like I wasn't sure what I was going to do with my life. I was so scared for so long; scared of Adam, scared of making a mistake and him hurting me. I wasn't scared anymore. Adam was going to be locked up and regardless, Elijah was here to protect me.

The rest of our picnic was filled with a mixture of conversation, laughing, and kissing. The latter being my favourite part. If Theo noticed the change in dynamic between the two of us, he didn't say anything. He was only little; I don't think he was thinking much past the amount of fun he was having. When the sun started to set, we packed everything back into Elijah's truck and headed home. My hand rested in Elijah's the whole time as I turned to see a sleeping Theo behind us.

"That kid falls asleep so easily," Elijah joked.

"He gets it from me, I think," I said, chuckling.

"Lucas is staying at Ma's tonight." I wondered if that was a coincidence or if Elijah had asked him to.

"Do you think he would be okay with Theo staying in his room?"

"He won't mind. Besides, it would mean I would at least have some warning before Theo throws himself on me first thing in the morning." I laughed at that. When we pulled up, Elijah got Theo out of the truck, careful not to wake him up. I made coffee whilst he took him up to Lucas' room.

"All good?" I asked as he came back down the stairs.

"Kid's out like a light."

Forty-Two

Elijah

I might have bribed Lucas to be elsewhere this evening. It was worth it so we could get some alone time together. I wasn't pushing for anything specific, I just didn't want to have to share Charlie's attention with anyone else. I don't care how selfish that sounds.

Theo falling asleep early was an added bonus I wasn't expecting. I grabbed the coffee she had made me and leaned against the counter next to her. She knocked my mug with hers in a mock cheer.

"Can we do things like today more often?" she asked, leaning into me. "I've always wanted to be the kind of person who does family picnics." I smiled, thinking back to my thoughts yesterday about wanting family walks together.

"Of course we can. I better arrange with Theo to go fishing otherwise he's going to pester me till the end of time." She threw her head back with a laugh.

"He will absolutely love that." I put down my cup and turned so I was facing her. Her arms came around my neck and I leaned down to kiss her. My intention was to be soft, but I quickly found myself getting carried away. This was first moment we had properly been alone since the gala. I lifted her onto the counter, our lips still exploring. Her hands tugged at my shirt as she lifted it up and over my head. My hands slid down, resting on her legs before I hesitated.

"Don't stop," she said breathlessly.

"Are you sure?" I was conscious of her comment yesterday. "We don't have to rush into anything."

"I'm one hundred percent certain, Elijah." Her mouth met mine once more.

* * *

I woke up before Charlie the next morning, our bodies intertwined in my bed. My mind kept playing reruns of last night. I didn't make a habit of sleeping around, but I wasn't exactly celibate, either. Being with Charlie was different. For the first time, there were feelings wrapped up in it. Usually, I favoured one-night stands purely to satisfy mutual needs, but this was different. This was more than just sex with her. I felt her start to stir next to me as her eyes slowly opened.

"Morning, Officer Sunshine," she said, adjusting herself to be closer.

"Morning." I placed a kiss on top of her head. "How'd you sleep?"

"Like a log." She chuckled lightly. "I guess I was pretty tired last night."

"I wonder why," I quipped. She blushed at my words.

"We should probably get dressed; Theo will be awake soon." I groaned, but she was right. I forced myself out of my comfortable position, searching my drawer for an outfit to put on. "What time are you going to work?" she asked as made her way over to her bag.

"In a couple hours." It was her chance to groan now.

"Don't feel like calling in sick today and spending the day with us?"

"I hope you're not planning on being a bad influence on me, Charlotte." She laughed as I kissed her, pressing her against the wall.

"I know you have to work, I'll just miss you, that's all. I feel like we are just getting used to being around each other."

"What are your plans for today?" I ask in an attempt to slightly change the subject. I was genuinely worried that if she carried on, I would in fact call in sick.

"Not a lot, I need to go back to my place, really." I gave her a look in an attempt to say *no you don't*. "I need some more clothes!" She hit me playfully. "There is also a lack of toys around here and Theo needs more than just cartoons to keep him occupied."

"Would you rather I came to yours tonight?" I hadn't really accounted for the fact that this house wasn't exactly equipped for a three-year-old. I made a mental note to have a look at buying some things for Theo to play with whilst he was here. Besides, it wouldn't be fair of me to kick Lucas out for a second night in a row.

"You think we are going to spend tonight together, too?" She folded her arms over her chest. I felt a mild sense of guilt that I had just assumed we would spend the night together. I didn't particularly want to sleep alone again. "I'm kidding, I'm happy for you to come over tonight. Only if you don't mind, that is."

"Of course not. I'll pack a bag now and come straight from work." She kissed my cheek before leaving the room to check on Theo. Pancake breakfasts were seemingly becoming a tradition in my house now. I wasn't sure it was a sustainable breakfast to upkeep forever, but they were sacred to me now. A couple hours later we were saying a begrudging goodbye as I headed into work and they headed home. Knowing I would be coming back to them later was the only thing getting me through today.

Daines had the stupidest grin on his face when I walked into work that afternoon. Although, I also had a pretty big grin on my face, too, after my day with Charlie and Theo yesterday.

"So, when's the wedding?" he teased. I know he was joking, but the thought of marrying Charlie one day made my heart pound. Nobody had ever made me feel like this before. I was obsessed with how happy she made me feel.

"Shut it." I elbowed him as I walked past, prompting a laugh from him.

"She makes you happy?" he asked more seriously now.

"Very." Daines always knew exactly how much to pry and when to leave it alone. He didn't ask me any more questions after that and he didn't push me for details. I was grateful for it. He knew better than anyone that I would talk about it when I was ready.

As we finished the pre-check, I felt my phone buzz in my pocket.

Lucas: I had to listen to Ma ask me about my dating life all

night. I hope you made the night of the house to yourself worth it.

Elijah: Very.

I laughed as I put it back in my pocket, Daines raised an eyebrow at me.

"I asked Lucas if he could give me the house to myself yesterday." Daines interrupted me with a wolf whistle. "He was just saying Ma was giving him grief about his dating life. She can be a bit much sometimes."

"Hey!" he said sternly. "Your mother is a great lady. Don't you boys give her any grief, you hear me?" I held my hands up defensively. Daines had unintentionally seemed to step into a father figure role for us siblings. He'd always been close with my dad and our family, but my father's death seemed to bring him closer. He lost his wife a few years after dad died, too, and I think he needed us just as much as we needed him.

"I think because she was married young, she is impatient for all of us to get married." I shrugged as I got into the car with Daines climbing into the driver's seat.

"I guess retrospectively it wasn't a bad thing they met young," he said softly. "In the end, it meant they got more time together." I'd never really thought about it that way before. It was hard to talk about my dad, but I felt more comfortable talking about him with Daines. He knew my dad more or less his entire life, it helped me feel closer to him. We sat quietly for a second as Daines started to pull away for a drive round.

"Do you think he'd be disappointed?" I don't know where I found the courage to ask, but I found myself wishing I could take the words back.

"Of you?" he asked and I answered him with a nod.

"Your dad was my best friend in the whole world, Eli. I loved him like a brother." He sniffed. "So, you better believe me when I say, all your dad ever wanted was for you three kids to be happy. He would be so damn proud of the man you are." I tried to choke back my tears, but a few strayed down my face. Daines hand landed on my shoulder as he pulled into a layby.

"I am so proud of the man you are," he said, squeezing my shoulder. "I asked to be your partner not because you were my best friend's son, but because you are the bravest person I know. You were fifteen and you ran straight after that guy who killed your dad without a second thought. If you had cowered in the corner, I wouldn't have blamed you, but you didn't you fought back. You're a fighter, Elijah, just like he was." He cleared his throat in an attempt to hide the emotion in his voice.

"It was my fault." I wasn't able to hide the emotion in my voice as I bit back a sob.

"How was it your fault?" I looked up at Daines, there was genuine confusion in his face.

"I heard the noise downstairs, but I ignored it. I had a gut feeling something was wrong, but I didn't go. I got scared." I could feel my breath getting unsteady. "If I had gone down when I first heard it then it would have been me who spooked the robber and got shot instead of Dad. I couldn't even catch him after."

He was quiet for a moment and I searched to see if I could see the disappointment in his face.

"It wasn't your fault, Elijah."

"It was—"

"No. It wasn't." He sighed. "If you tell your ma I told you this, I'm going to be in a load of trouble." I looked at him confused. "That man wasn't an ordinary robber; your father was working on a big case against an organised crime group. That intruder was a man they sent; he never had any intention of letting James live through it. If you had gone down first, we would have lost both of you."

I let his words sink in for a moment. I tried to wrap my head around the gravity of the information I had just been given. I knew my father was a criminal defence lawyer who worked big cases in the city, but I never paid much attention to the cases themselves.

"But they never caught the guy who did it? How would they know he was sent by the gang?" He had slipped my grasp and the rest of the Rosehaven PD. It had bothered me for years that the man who killed my father was still out there.

"They didn't need to catch him to know. James had been receiving threats for weeks. I told him to report it or drop the case, but he wouldn't." Daines sighed again. I could tell it was painful for him to relive, but I was glad he told me. I still held onto some guilt, but I felt a small weight lifted off my chest knowing that there wouldn't have been anything I could have done to stop it. At the same time, I felt frustrated that there wasn't anything I could have done about it.

"Your father was a good man, but he died because of a poor decision he made. He would be devasted if he knew that you had been blaming yourself all of these years. If Lucas came in and told you he felt responsible for your father's death because he heard the robber and was slow to respond, what would you say to him?"

Daines had me there. "I'd tell him it wasn't his fault." I sighed.

Forty-Three

Charlotte

I can't believe it had taken me this long to leave Adam and move on with my life. He was still slightly lingering, but I felt freer than I had done in years. Elijah ticked every box for me and seemed to be occupying any free space in my head at the moment.

Theo was skipping along beside me as we walked home. I almost felt like skipping, too. It wasn't too long of a walk and I could do with the fresh air.

"Mommy, when are we going to play at Elijah and Lucas' house again?" he asked.

"Elijah's actually coming to play at our house tonight." Theo beamed. I felt a squeeze in my chest at his question. He seemed to genuinely enjoy spending time with them and it made me happy. I hoped we were going to be spending a lot more time with them and it was important to me that Theo was happy with that.

No matter what, he would always come first.

"Do you like Elijah?" I asked cautiously as we walked along.

"He's one of my best friends," Theo said happily. I ruffled my hand in his hair. That was exactly what I wanted to hear. Elijah was always kind and gentle with Theo, he was a natural at it. It seemed so effortless the way he interacted with Theo. The rest of the Weatherstons were brilliant with him, too. I loved this new family we had found ourselves with. When my parents cut me off, I thought I had lost my chance at having a family. Now here I was a few years later, having found a completely new one. The Weatherstons had accepted me immediately as one of their own and I was grateful to them. I looked forward to continue to get to know each and every single one of them. I looked forward to summer BBQs, birthdays, and Christmases with them. I looked forward to finally feeling like I belonged somewhere.

When we walked up to the front door of my apartment, I spotted the window of Theo's room was open. I must have forgotten to close it a few days ago when we left. I cursed myself for being reckless, I was lucky something bad hadn't happened. Theo ran ahead of me as we walked in. I saw him freeze when he entered the living room.

"Daddy?" he asked his voice shaking. My heart dropped when I walked in the room and saw Adam sitting at the kitchen table.

"Where have you been, Lottie?" His voice was cold. He was supposed to be locked up. How was he here?

"Theo, can you go in the bedroom, sweetheart? Maybe take some of your cars with you?" I pushed his shoulders lightly, nudging him towards his bedroom. He obliged, but looked back of me before he closed the door. I could sense how unsure he was.

"Where have you been, Lottie?" Adam asked again after Theo was gone.

"At a friend's house." I don't know why I was explaining myself to him. I felt like I did before I left, like I needed to answer his every wish. That I owed him an explanation to my every move.

"With Elijah Weatherston?" There was a bitterness in his voice as he said his name. I didn't realise he even knew Elijah's name, but I guess after the arrest it wouldn't have been hard for him to figure out. "You didn't take long to move on from me, playing house with your little police officer boyfriend. Did you think that would keep you safe from me?" I felt the hairs on my neck stand up on edge.

I was still stood in the same spot as when I first entered, unable to move myself.

"You need to leave, Adam." He rose from his seat and moved closer to me. I reached in my pocket for my phone, but Adam reached his arm out and smacked it out of my hand. Bringing his leg up, he stomped on it multiple times and I watched it crumble beneath his feet.

"You are going to go in that room, pack a bag, and we are going to go home, Lottie." He grabbed my wrist, shoving me forcefully towards the bedroom. I knew I wasn't going to be able to call Elijah to get me out of this situation. I was going to have to get myself out of this one myself. I turned sharply towards him.

"No!" I yelled as loudly as I could.

I don't think I had ever said the word *no* to Adam before. There was something exhilarating about standing up to him. "You are going to turn around and leave my house. Now,

Adam." I held my ground even though I was terrified. I wasn't going to let him push me around not anymore. He was not about to take everything away from me. I was never going to let him take anything from me ever again.

"Enough! Don't you dare speak to me like that." He spat back at me, pushing my back against the wall by the kitchen. His hand slapped me hard across my cheek, I fought the tears that threatened to come. I wasn't going to give him the satisfaction of seeing me cry. "You are *nothing*, Lottie, do you understand? You are *worthless* without me." His words hurt more than his fists. There was a part of me that used to believe him. Whenever he would tell me that before I agreed with him, I did feel worthless without him. That was until I met Elijah. In the few weeks I'd known him, he'd made me feel important. He'd made me feel cared for and special, like I meant something. All I've ever wanted was to mean something to someone.

"You don't scare me, Adam." I held my ground. His hand came to my throat and I thrashed my arms against him to try to get him to loosen his grip. I felt my breathing restrict as I struggled again him. I managed to get a good kick in him and he loosened his grip on me. With frustration, he threw me to the ground before walking into the kitchen. Once I caught my breath I screamed. I screamed as loudly as I could. I needed to try to alert my neighbours' attention to my situation.

"Shut up." he yelled, pinning me on the floor. "You're not getting away from me this time." His hand came over my mouth as I tried to keep screaming. "Why can't you see that I'm doing this because I love you? You're making it harder for yourself." I stopped fighting and he loosened his grip on me. A moment later I kicked out as hard as I could, pushing him off me as I scrambled towards the kitchen. When I got to my feet I grabbed a knife from the butcher block.

"Leave, Adam! Now!" I held it out shakily towards him. I was not a violent person, but there was nothing I wouldn't do to protect Theo. *Nothing.* Adam jumped towards me and I swiped the knife at him, but I missed. He grabbed my wrist, turning it until I dropped it and pushed me away from it. I let the tears fall as I watched him pick up the knife and walk towards me.

He embraced me as he plunged the knife into me, whispering "This is all your fault, Lottie. Maybe I should start punishing our son to keep you in line." I tried to bite back my scream, but I couldn't. Yelling out in pain as he pulled the knife back out of my stomach before launching it in again. I knew if I didn't start fighting back, I was a goner. I couldn't let him get to Theo. I thrashed again, trying to grapple onto the knife and failing. We wrestled for a few minutes as I tried to overpower him and failed. I managed to dig my nails into the side of his neck and he screamed out in pain, backing away from me. The break was short-lived as he swung the knife into my arm and I yelled out in pain. He stood up, staring down at me.

"This could have been so much easier, Lottie. If you had come with me none of this would have happened you know." He rubbed his neck. "Why couldn't you just do what you're told?" he yelled. I was stuck on the floor now, unable to move myself at all.

There was a crash and I heard the sound of footsteps through the door. I couldn't focus my eyes on the room as I felt them getting heavy.

Forty-Four

Elijah

∾∾∾

My phone rang and I turned it over to see Officer Taylor calling me. I don't think he's ever called me before.

"It wasn't my call, Elijah," he said immediately as I answered.

"What are you talking about?"

"They released Adam last night."

"They what? What do you mean they released him?" My voice raising as I spoke. "Why didn't they fucking charge him?"

"Not enough evidence."

"There were multiple witnesses!"

I couldn't contain my anger.

"I told you, it wasn't my call." I hung up the call, throwing my phone at the dash.

"What's going on?" Daines turned to me, eyebrows raised.

"Adam has been released. We need to go to Charlie's house. Now."

Our conversation was interrupted by radio chatter and my head snapped up.

Neighbours report of shouting and a woman in distress. The call followed with the address through the radio.

"That's Charlie's address," I whispered. Daines eyes widened as he turned on the siren and pulled out of the lay-by at speed. We didn't need to discuss whether or not we would be picking up that call. Charlie was in danger.

I couldn't speak.

My heart was pounding in my chest. I needed to get to her now, that was all I could think about. I needed her to be safe.

"We'll be there in a couple of minutes," Daines said in an attempt to reassure me. It didn't. What if we were a couple of minutes too late?

My heart was pounding as I busted through the door into her apartment. My eyes immediately scanned the room and saw Adam standing over her with a knife in his hand. He turned back towards the noise and smirked as we came in. Charlotte was on the floor in a pool of blood and my heart dropped. Rushing over, I threw myself at Adam, knocking the knife out of his hands. I heard Daines move then towards the knife, kicking it far out of Adam's reach. Adam and I wrestled on the floor as I struggled to grab hold of his arms. I felt a smack against my head as he swung one of Theos toy's against my skull, sending me off of him. He climbed on top of me and swung it down again. Daines lifted Adam up by the arms, tossing him off me to the side. Adam kicked him hard, forcing him to the ground before turning and running out the door.

My eyes darted between the door and Charlie laying next to me, her eyes shut. "Go, you're faster than me. I've got Lottie!" Daines shouted at me as he crouched down. I got to my feet, running straight out the door after Adam. He had gotten a head start, but he was still in my sights. This was the reason I went running nearly every single day. When I was fifteen, I wasn't fast enough and the man who murdered my father got away. There was no way in hell Adam was going to get away from me. This time I would stop at nothing to catch the person I was chasing. He would pay dearly for hurting Charlie.

Adam was fast, but I was faster and soon I was gaining on him. He also didn't know these streets like I did. As I saw him round a corner, I dove down the alleyway to my right on the other side. He was within arm's reach and I took the leap, my arms grappling around his waist as I tackled him into someone's front lawn. He tried to fight, but I had the upper hand this time. I lifted my fist up before making contact with his face. I did it again, and again, and again. I felt like a man possessed as my hand kept beating down on his face. Blood was pouring out, but it didn't stop me. After a few more hits and I was certain he wasn't going to fight back anymore, I found it within me to stop. He groaned as he clutched his face.

"I warned you about touching what was mine." I spat on the ground next to him. Officers Taylor and Lawrence were making their way over as I stood.

"Cuff him." Both were looking at me wide-eyed as his blood trickled off my knuckles.

"I expect to see that I had to use self-defence on a violent criminal on the report." I eyed them both and they nodded as they went to pick him up. I picked up my pace and ran back towards Charlie's place, anxious to get back and make she was okay. I walked in the room where she was still laid on the floor. My eyes were drawn to the blood. There's so much blood. I tried to steady myself on the wall as flashes of my father came to mind. I felt my breathing quicken.

"Elijah…" Her voice broke my trance as I rushed over to her side. She looked like she was in pain, but there was still a gentle smile on her face.

"Don't you dare go anywhere, Charlie. Don't you dare leave me." I gripped her hand tightly. "I already lost someone like this, I can't lose you, too. I can't do it, Charlie."

"I already told you that you were stuck with me, Officer Sunshine." Paramedics entered the room and Officer Daines moved out the way to let them through.

"Where's Theo?" I frantically looked around the room.

"He's probably hiding under the bed. I always told him to do that when he was frightened by the yelling." *Jesus Christ.* I made eye contact with Daines who nodded and made his way into the bedroom to look for him.

"We need to move her onto the trolley," one of the paramedics said. I moved backwards to let them work. My eyes didn't leave her for a moment. Theo emerged from the room then.

"Mommy!" he yelled as he tried to run towards her. I caught him before he ran into the paramedics. My chest ached as I looked at his face, at the fear consuming it. I was reminded of Lucas and Alice when they were on the stairs watching as my father died. I remember this look from their faces. The outcome would be different for Theo, though. I was sure of it. He had just lost his father in roundabout kind of way; I wasn't going to watch him lose his mother, too.

"It's okay, Theo, these guys are helping Mommy." I steadied myself as I reached for his hands. "You trust me, don't you?" He nodded, tears running down his cheeks. My eyes moved briefly to Charlie as they wheeled her out of the front door. She had to be okay, she just had to be. "I promise you, everything is going to be okay. They are going to take her to the hospital and make her all better." I'm not sure who I was trying to convince here, me or him. I picked up Theo and we walked out the front of the house. I saw Alice running towards us as her eyes widened with horror at Charlie being loaded into the ambulance.

"Oh, Eli." She hugged my tightly, giving Theo a kiss on the head. "I'll give you a ride to the hospital." Daines came up behind.

"I'll do it. I can use the sirens to get us there quicker," he interrupted. We hustled over to the car. I was grateful Daines was driving because my hands were shaking as we drove along, my eyes fixated on the ambulance in front of me. *Was she still alive in there?* I thought back to the blood flowing out of her when she was on the floor, she had still been talking to me. Then again so had my dad at first when he got shot.

We were ushered into the waiting room as soon as we got to the hospital. I needed to be strong for Theo and that was the only reason I wasn't falling apart right now. He needed me to hold it together. They rushed Charlie straight into surgery and we all sat for hours in that room. Alice and I tried at different points to make light of everything for Theo, but he hardly said a word. The boy who was always chatting and laughing was frozen in shock. Alice had nearly bitten every single one of her nails in the time we were waiting. A couple hours or so in, Lucas appeared.

"I'm so sorry, I had my phone off." He rushed in, hugging us each in turn. "How is she?" I shook my head.

"She's still in surgery will be for a while yet, I think," Alice said, quickly returning to biting her nails. Lucas joined us in sitting and we waited again in silence. Theo eventually fell asleep leaning against Lucas. It was another couple of tense hours before a doctor walked in.

"Elijah?" Her eyes looked straight at me. "Can you come with me, please?" All eyes were on me as I followed the doctor out of the room.

Forty-Five

Charlotte

There were flickers of memories. I saw Elijah leaning over me begging me not to leave him. I heard Theo calling me. I felt myself being whisked away, my eyes staring straight at the sky. The next time I opened my eyes I was in a hospital bed. The room was bright and I had to close my eyes again briefly whilst I adjusted. I tried to move my body, but I felt a pain in my stomach and arm as I did so. I remembered now, how I got here. Adam wielding the knife over me, stabbing it into me. I relived that moment over and over again until a nurse walked in.

"You're awake," she said cheerfully. "Let me just get the doctor." She rushed out of the room as quickly as she walked in. She was followed a few moments later by a doctor and they set about checking me over.

"Is Elijah here?" I asked after a while. The nurse said there were a few people waiting for me.

"Is he a police officer?" I nodded. "Yes, he's out in the waiting room."

"Would I be able to see him?"

"Of course, we will get him for you when we've finished." I took a breath, allowing my eyes to close briefly whilst they finished looking me over. A few moments later, the doctor walked back in with Elijah in tow.

"Charlie." He rushed quickly to my side, his hands hovering over me like he was scared to touch me.

"Hey, Officer Sunshine." I smiled weakly at him. "You can touch me, I'm a lot stronger than you give me credit for."

"I know you are," he said, placing his hand lightly on my side. "How are you feeling?"

"A little bruised, but I'll be okay." I paused taking him in. He looked exhausted, but then I think I probably looked a little worse for wear as well. "I stood up to him, Elijah. For the first time in my life, I stood up for myself." He looked at me and smiled, squeezing my hand gently.

"That's my girl." His thumb rubbed over the back of my hand. "Thank you for not leaving me."

"We're just barely getting started, I am not going anywhere." He looked at me for a minute and I met his gaze. "Are you okay?" I watched as he took a deep breath.

"I'm better because of you, Charlie."

"What do you mean by that?"

"I've spent the past fifteen years barely hanging on. I always had this niggling voice in the back of my head telling me just to wait. That something better was coming and I needed to hold on for it." He took a deep breath before continuing. "I know now that the voice was telling me to wait for you, Charlie. You are the something better I always dreamed would come."

Seeing the tears forming in his eyes sent some down my own cheeks.

"I love you, Charlotte Miller," he said, pulling my hand to his lips and kissing it. "Meeting you was the best thing that ever happened to me."

"I love you, too." He leaned over the bed and kissed me. He was soft as he did so, his hand gently caressing my face.

"Are you up for seeing Theo?" he asked.

"Please." He smiled and walked out of the room. Theo ran into the room a short while later.

"Mommy!" he squealed. Elijah quickly grabbed him before he jumped on the bed.

"Careful, buddy, Mommy is still healing, remember?" Elijah reminded him before gently placing him next to me.

"I thought you said they were going to fix her up?"

"They have, darling," I said, holding his hand in mine. "I'm just going to be a little sore for a couple of days."

"Is Daddy gone now? He's not going to hurt Mommy again, is he?" Theo asked, his attention on Elijah.

"Your daddy will never come near your mom again. He's been arrested and he will be going to prison for a long time." I couldn't help but feel relieved that Adam was locked away, this time for good. He wasn't going to hurt us anymore. Elijah moved close, kissing Theo on the forehead and then me on the lips.

"I love you both so much. Things are going to be better from now on, I promise." Both Theo and I beamed. "How would you feel about moving into my place?" He posed this question to me now. "I'd like to have you close to me."

"What do you reckon, Theo? Do you want to move in to Elijah's house?" He looked at me, his face still beaming.

"I'd love it! Can I bring my toys?"

"You can bring whatever you want, buddy. What about you, Charlie?"

"There is nothing I'd want more."

Throughout the next couple of hours, the Weatherstons popped in to visit me. Alice cuddled me and promised me a girl's night out when I was feeling better. Lucas offered to have Theo at the shop for a few days to help him with cars whilst I was recovering. Lucy brought me some home baked goods with the promise of a family dinner. I was overwhelmed with the outpouring of love in this hospital room.

It was a few days before I was released from hospital. Elijah stayed by my side as much as possible until I was discharged. In my absence, Lucas and Alice had spent time decorating parts of Elijah's house to make it more of a home. There were loads of toys for Theo and a little play area set aside for him. I was blown away by their kindness.

I stood in the kitchen taking in the view as Elijah wrapped his arms around me, the sound of Lucas and Theo playing in the background. I looked out and thought of my grandpa.

I found him Grandpa. I thought to myself as Elijah kissed my neck. *I found the person who treats me like you treated Grandma. Thank you for reminding me not to settle for less.*

Forty-Six

Elijah

6 Months Later- EPILOGUE

I only made it six weeks after that night in the hospital before I popped the question to Charlie, with Theo's permission, of course. I was more nervous to ask him than I was his mother. After everything that happened with his dad, I was worried he would be protective over Charlie and not want anyone to burst their safety bubble. When I spoke to him, the first thing he asked was if he could have a swing set in the backyard. That boy could have a whole damn playground if it meant I got to keep him and Charlie in my life permanently.

If it was up to me, I would have taken Charlie to the courthouse the second she said yes, but she wanted to wait and plan a wedding.

I wanted to have a quiet wedding at a courthouse while

she wanted a bigger wedding with all our friends and family. We compromised and planned a big wedding with all of our friends and family. As long as I was around, Charlie would get everything she ever wanted. There was nothing I wouldn't do to keep a smile on her face.

She brought out parts of me that had been buried for years, some parts of me I never knew existed at all. Our house was filled with music at all times and I loved it. She loved me despite all of my faults and my anxieties. A couple weeks after we left the hospital, she helped me find a therapist to talk through a lot of my guilt around losing my dad. Talking about him and what happened helped better than I ever could ever have imagined. For years, I refused to talk about him at all. It was definitely an adjustment to then talk about it with a stranger, no less. Charlie came with me to every single session; I don't think I could have done it without her. It felt good to talk about him, not just the bad stuff but the good, too. At family dinners we spoke about him, talked about all the good times with him. Sometimes I felt like he was in the room with us. He would have loved Charlie and Theo. I know that for certain.

After I started going to therapy, I visited his grave. I hadn't been there since the funeral. I wanted to apologise to him, I knew now that it wasn't my fault.

I was just a kid. If I had taken on that attacker, there was every chance I'd be six feet under, too. I went to apologise to him for wasting the years after. He may have been the one who died, but I was the one who stopped living. I promised him I would change that, I would no longer waste days like I used to. I would make the most of all the moments I had left, every moment with my new family. I knew now I had no way of controlling everything, only how I react to it. I wished it hadn't taken me fifteen years to realise that.

I always thought I'd be freaked out on my wedding day. Maybe I'd get cold feet and Lucas would have to talk me down. I couldn't have been more wrong. Today is the best day of my life. Today is the day Charlie Miller is going to become my wife. The girls were all staying the night before at my mother's house, so it was just Lucas, Theo, and I at home. We had converted my old office into Theo's room temporarily. Lucas had been fixing up the apartment above his auto shop to move into, so Theo would be moving into his room soon. I told Lucas there was no rush to leave, but he kindly informed me the walls were pretty thin and he was quite happy to move out and give us our space.

I was the first person down in the morning. My eyes lingering over my piano as I drank my coffee. I used to play to calm myself down, but now I play because I enjoy it. Sitting down I allowed my fingers to play a few keys to pass the time before the morning really began.

It wasn't long until both Lucas and Theo were downstairs and we were getting dressed into our suits. Lucas was cat walking up and down the hallway in his.

"You know, this is definitely the sexiest I have ever looked," he said as he paused to look at himself in the mirror. I rolled my eyes and continued to help Theo with his tie. Soon, we were all ready and just waiting for the car to pick us up.

"You feeling good?" Lucas asked me. "No cold feet?"

"My feet aren't even a little bit cold," I said, shaking my head. I reached into my pocket, making sure the picture was still there as I pulled it out. My eyes looked directly in my fathers in the picture. I turned it round to show Lucas. He responded by pulling a copy of another photo out of his own pocket making me smile.

"Alice, Ma, and Charlie have one in their necklaces, too," he said.

"I wish he was here for this." I sucked in a breath.

"He is here for it, Eli. We're all carrying him around so he can see all of it. He's not going to miss a thing, I promise." The pictures were Charlie's idea. She and I also had one of her grandparents on our persons, as well. She said if we carried their pictures around, it would be like they were with us. I wanted to believe that was true. I wanted more than anything to have him with me today. Lucas pulled me in for a hug and I held him tightly.

"I'm proud of you, Eli. I'm really happy for you. For both of you," he said as he pulled away.

"Thank you. Your time will be here before you know it," I teased.

"Yeah, right. I don't think I'll ever be getting married." He scoffed. "I'm happy being the cool, fun uncle to Violet and Theo." We all turned to face the door at the sound of a car pulling up.

"We all ready?" I asked.

"Ready," Theo and Lucas said in unison.

"Let's go get you married, big brother," Lucas said, slapping me on the back as he passed.

I waited as long as I could to head to the front of the altar. I wanted people's eyes on me as little as possible. I felt my phone buzz and pulled it out to turn it off, but the text caught my eye.

Alice: I bet you $100 that you're going to cry your eyes

out when you see how beautiful your bride is.
   Alice: Love you, Eli. You deserve this.

I couldn't wait to see her and it wasn't long until I got to. It felt like an out of body moment when the registrar asked everyone to stand. I was glad I didn't take that bet with Alice, because my wallet would have been $100 lighter. I had just about managed to pull myself together by the time we got to the vows.

I cleared my throat before speaking, my hands in Charlie's. I didn't think she could get more beautiful, but here she was.

"You showed me a letter not long after we first met that your grandpa wrote," I began. I was nervous at all the people listening and looking at me, but I kept my breath steady. I kept my focus on her. "He asked you not to settle for any less than you deserve, to be with someone who would fight to make you happy, to make you smile." I let out a breath before continuing.

"Charlie, I promise you that I will spend every single day of my life giving you everything you deserve. I will fight to keep that smile on your face. You and Theo are my world." I turned to look at Theo standing next to Lucas. "You know as well as I do that life is short, but I plan on making the most of every single minute life gives me with you. I love you, Charlie, and I always will."

Acknowledgements

Firstly to all of the readers, thank you for taking the time to read my debut novel Read My Rights. Becoming a published author has been a lifelong dream of mine and I am honoured that it is now a reality.

Within every story I write you will find a piece of me. Often in life we feel alone in our struggles, I hope through reading Elijah and Charlotte's stories you find comfort. Your struggles do not make you any less deserving of love.

To Tom, your support with this as with everything was unwavering. Thank you for your patience and encouragement as I spent many hours shut away writing this story.

To my family and friends, thank you for never lessening my sparkle.

To Alessia, Nay and Iqqy. From the moment I spoke this book into existence you have put the entire weight of your support behind me. Thank you for listening to my endless ramblings and allowing me to lean on you when I needed it. You helped this book become the finished work that it is.

To my ARC Readers/Street Team, thank you for taking a chance on me and for being a vital part of spreading the word about my book.

To my editor Hannah, thank you for helping me find confidence in my writing. Your live commenting never failed to make me laugh.

To Brittany, thank you for bringing my characters to life through your beautiful cover.

Printed in Great Britain
by Amazon

43143655R00158